Dedication

I wish to give credit to all the people who passed through my life, each leaving behind their own little bit of the big mass of fragments that finally merged into this novel, *Mount Everest*. But it's really my wife, Mary Beth, who deserves full credit. Traveling together through the years of learning, struggling, trying, failing, and the score of simply unimaginable ups and downs, the bond between us held fast through everything. She was always there, encouraging, reassuring, and loving me through all the years; and I her. Without Mary Beth there would have been no writing, no books, no family, no nothing; in fact there would have been simply no value to be derived from my having lived at all.

Montag Press
ISBN: 978-1-940233-26-0
Cover art © 2015 Elena Vizerskaya
Cover, layout, & e-book © 2015 Sean Barnes

Montag Press Team:
Project Editor – Charlie Franco
Managing Director – Charlie Franco

A Montag Press Book
www.montagpress.com
Montag Press
1066 47th Ave. Unit #9
Oakland CA 94601 USA

Montag Press, the burning book with the hatchet cover, the skewed word mark and the portrayal of the long-suffering fireman mascot are trademarks of Montag Press.

Printed & Digitally Originated in the United States of America
10 9 8 7 6 5 4 3 2 1

MOUNT EVEREST

A NOVEL
JIM MEIROSE

MONTAG

There's something Jim Meirose does when he writes, and its definitely 'the hard way.' As a reader you have to earn his sentences, one after the other, to get to the bliss, the ecstasy. In this case, it's the very top of Mount Everest. In life, it's the very top of an author's skill. It's the reason I published a chapbook of his years ago and it's the reason I still still love reading him, climbing that mountain.

Flannery O'Connor and Samuel Beckett aren't dead; they're just found each other in the mind of Jim Meirose. 'Mount Everest' takes grotesqueries and near-nihilistic fetishes and pours them into a nightmare that is sometimes funny, always vivid, and unexpectedly incisive. Surreal, scary, even scorching, 'Mount Everest' is a look at our trivial ambitions and pastoral fantasies, and the dreamscapes that tell us more about reality than our waking hours ever could.

Jim Meirose's *Mount Everest* takes the reader on an orgiastic trip through the personal nightmare of two main characters. A mother and daughter find themselves caught in a web of hoarding and prostitution. The story of Thelma and Christine can only be described as gripping because Meirose portrays their plight with keen insight and compassion. Christine's scandalous activities dominate the action, but all within the context of the family history. The book contains valid psychological insights as the lead characters lapse into, and out of, flights of fantasy and delusion.

Thelma, who is in her mid-seventies, took up hoarding after her husband died. Her house has become the bane of the neighborhood, an eyesore that has the neighbors up in arms. Christine, who had been confined to a mental hospital for twenty years, supplements her mother's social security check with her own enterprise that she describes as "marriage counseling." Tension builds as inspectors and process servers slog through piles of garbage that have accumulated in and around the residence. Readers know that eviction and disaster is right around the corner for these two ladies.

The sections featuring Christine are interspersed with portraits of the "Johns" who visit the premises. These visitors serve as interpreters of the action that occurs under the same dismal roof in the Nebraska town. The author draws a fine line between Christine's pathology and the apparent sanity of her admirers. The "Johns" come across, as did Christine and Thelma, as human characters with authentic emotional responses. Especially memorable are these clients' reveries of their experiences with Christine. The author treats all the characters with understanding and humanity.

Mount Everest displays an unconventional style but is extremely clear once the reader understands the frequent stream of the consciousness point of view. It works. The words almost disappear as we are drawn into the narrative. The book is compelling because it is so easy to identify with the characters and their plight. It is like looking at the inevitable train wreck happening before our eyes. We cannot look away. The reader's interest will probably not flag in this book (a characteristic of so many current novels with good premises but not much follow through). Eventually, *Mount Everest* does come to a fitting conclusion. One does not have to struggle to reach the final page, but the reader will feel sorry the drama has come to an end.

— G.A. Ivins,
author of *The Homicidal Detective*.

Mount Everest mines one of the more popular of twenty-first century literary territories, the off-beat, slightly spooky zone between reality and madness, but thanks to a seamless blending of content and deftly-controlled voice, Jim Meirose manages to make this satirical, fantastical Never-Never Land uniquely and engrossingly his own.

— Neal Storrs,
editor, *Oasis, a Literary Magazine*

In a house moldering in trash, a young woman wades through her own delusions, as she earns her living being used and discarded like the refuse around her. At every turn, Meirose forces you to feel the weight of our own consumption and the need to make our world clean.

— Trevor Richardson,
author of *Dystopia Boy* and editor of *The Subtopian*

MOUNT EVER3ST

A NOVEL

JIM MEIROSE

To my Grandson, Henry Heber

1 – Christine and Leandra

Two women stood facing each other between the mounds of trash. Trash of every shape, color, size and type filled not only the kitchen but was piled high in every room of the house. Trash that stank and crawled with critters. The two stood in the stench of the kitchen, a table heaped with trash between them, and talked. A notice from the town that had been pinned to the front door now lay on top of the mound.

So what are you going to do? Christine Zidar said, her finger on the notice. They say they're coming to inspect in two weeks. How are you going to get this place cleaned?

Nosy damned neighbors, Thelma half-whispered. It's the nosy God-Damned neighbors' fault. To hell with the Zidars. They say—they've always said to hell with the Zidars.

Mom. Mom—they've kind of got a reason. If the trash wasn't also spread across the front porch and in the yard, they'd never have complained. It doesn't matter now though—you've got two weeks before the inspector comes. What are you going to do?

Nothing, the old woman said —your Father wouldn't let himself be pushed around like this. We've gotten notices before—we've always appealed—

But this one says final notice, Christine blurted—one last final notice before they evict us. The other ones never said final notice.

Final is meaningless. This is the United States. They can't just throw us out of our house in the United States. This is my house. All paid off too—paid off long ago!

As the old lady talked she remembered when she and Martin had bought the house when Christine was just eighteen months old. It was a beautifully kept, three-story, Victorian, in the best neighborhood of little Deshler, Nebraska, with an immaculate yard and a huge front porch, on a street lined with houses all just as impressive as hers. They had gotten it at a good price too—the realtor had said the prices were lower than they'd been in years before and that it was the perfect time to buy such a wonderful house. The old wealthy families were dying off and moving out to bigger houses in the suburbs and the neighborhood was slowly being replaced by working class families like her own. The houses were all beautiful back then, and she and Martin had happily moved in.

This is my house. It's paid off and I got the deed, Christine—I got the God-damned deed—they can't kick me out.

Christine raised her hand, understanding the old lady's point.

The deed isn't a license to turn a house into a trash dump Mom. We can't blame the neighbors for complaining about the way you've let this place go. The house, the yard—it looks like they've been God-damned abandoned for Christ's sake—how do you think I feel when I have somebody over here? How do you think I feel Mom?

Those are Johns you have over. That's nothing to brag about—

At least they bring in money to keep food on the table! What about you? You aren't bringing in anything—

I've got my pension—

Yeah! Five hundred a month from that dress factory you worked at. Still, even with your job, after Pop died, you let this place go to hell—

Martin was a heating contractor. To the day, one year after they moved into the house, he fell asleep at the wheel of his red pickup truck, ran into a ditch, flipped over, and the roof of his truck crushed down onto him. They said he died instantly. Christine was three when it happened. After that Thelma got a job at the big dress factory up in Hebron while her daughter spent her days at the cheapest day care they could afford. The day care center they chose for her in Deshler was a pigpen, a wooden box for working people's children, left for eight hours at a time. It was all that Thelma could afford. Christine spent her days playing alone on the day care center's rubber mats with the broken plastic toys, ignored by people her mother called staff. Smelly and dirty, the other children stayed away from her. Even though Martin was only shortly dead, Thelma was already letting her daughter and the house they shared go to seed. Something happened in her after Martin was killed in his tumbling red truck. When the trash started to accumulate in each of their rooms, Christine thought nothing of it, because being so young, it was all she knew.

It was when she went to Deshler elementary school, at the age of five, that her troubles began. Thelma had sent her child with filthy hands and face to school in too-tight outgrown clothing covered in a smell that was nothing short of outrageous. Because of this, no one would play with her and her teachers kept their distance whispering to themselves with sideways glances. As the years passed Christine began to suspect that something was wrong; she could feel that she was different from all the other kids. School became no place she wanted to be so she began going instead to places in her mind. With her house a hell, and her school a hell, the places in her mind were quiet, soft, calm, clean and bright. She spent her time there, adrift, until finally the teachers agreed that there was clearly something very wrong with her, and this is how she ended up in the big mental hospital all the way out in Omaha, at the age of ten, diagnosed with a mental disorder whose name her Mother couldn't pronounce. Even at the hospital, Christine was never really there; instead, like she had done before, she went to other places in her mind; places in the springtime with grassy rolling hills and puffy trees, places with flowers and sweetly chirping birds; to everyone else, the doctors, nurses and orderlies, she was said to be catatonic.

—at least I bring in a few hundred dollars a week Mom—you can't deny that. I keep us going. Yes! Me! I! I keep us going.

Yes but how? How? The way you keep us going, you should be ashamed—

No, Mom. You are the one who should be ashamed. Look at this place—can't you see it? We live like all the trash that you have stuffed in here.

It was in her dreams in the hospital where Christine met Leandra. Leandra had come down from the horizon in a grassy sunny place where Christine was and had come up to her smiling. When she got to Christine, Leandra even didn't have to say her name. Christine already knew what it was. She had risen from her sitting position on the grassy slope and faced Leandra who had a single freckle on the very tip of her nose.

I am sick, Christine had told Leandra.

You are? What do you have? Can I catch it?

I don't think so.

Then let's walk. You've been sitting here on this grass for too long.

Together, in Christine's mind, they walked for the first time along a pebbly path between two wide deep green gardens.

You know, Christine had said—I've been here since I was ten.

Oh? I've always been here. Isn't it beautiful?

The sun had slanted down around them, the gardens lush and full.

No—I don't mean here. I mean in the hospital.

I know. I left the hospital years ago.

You did? How?

I died.

Christine remembers feeling a wave of fear crawl up her back but it had dissipated before it could get into her brain. That way it could not get in and form thoughts that would've helped Christine leave the hospital. Instead, she just stayed in her gardens, walking under the branches of a peach tree that Leandra had pulled down to examine the leaves closely.

Look at all the veins, Leandra said clearly.

Christine looked at the leaf carefully. The veins branched out into branches and those branches branched out into branches and so on, maybe forever if you looked at it long enough; but Leandra just let the leaf flutter to the ground.

What are you going to do when they let you out?

I don't know, I don't think that they'll ever let me out of this place.

Oh sure they will. Just wait. When you go back there, do what they tell you and after enough time of doing what they tell you they will let you out. They let me out once.

Yes, but you—you died to get out. That's what you told me.

Aha! So I did. Well maybe not, that may have been a lie.

What?

Things are not always that simple—it is true I died—but that was just a way to get to someplace else.

Do you have to be dead to come to this place? Am I dead too? You could be—

Then as Christine remembers it, the ground was suddenly yanked out from underneath them and it rolled up and Leandra with it and in its place, the hospital room formed around Christine as she sat up for the first time in months in her bed. A nurse in the room, startled into attention, turned to Christine and said her name.

Christine? asked the nurse—you're awake—are you really awake? Can you see me?

Yes, I can. This is me. Really awake. Can you let me out of the hospital now?

But I was here to feed you—wait, just wait—I need to go get a doctor—

Christine was finally awake. For the first time since she could remember she felt alive, and alert, as the nurse rushed out. Many tests were then done, by many doctors, and she was found to be fine—and, a month later, she stood outside the hospital with her bag of clothes, waiting for her mother to come pick her up. She had so many questions for her mother. It had been raining while she had waited. Standing under the eaves of the stone archways she had gone over all the questions rushing about in her mind.

How old am I now?

How long was I sleeping?

How will I make my money?

Where will I live?

What kind of room will I have?

What kind of bed will be in it?

Where is Leandra?

When will I see her again?

Did she save me?

I feel I must love her.

Her mother had pulled up in a Lincoln car that floated on the long driveway like a big boat with a huge rusted out gash along its side. When she had gotten to the stone arches, she got out.

Christine! Christine, you're coming home, she had said hugging her daughter with a hug full of love. The way Leandra had. During that hug, she had thought that her mother must be a good woman. When mother had opened the door for Christine, Christine had got in ready to rejoin her life. She had thrown her bag into the back seat as her mother had gotten behind the wheel.

You've got to buckle up, she had said.

Buckle up? What do you mean?

Mother had showed her. Christine knew no more about such things than any other ten year old. Though her mind was that of a thirty year old there were many things that she didn't know. A lot of little things - little details that she had missed learning. Little details that taken together form what life is all about. When they had first gotten home from the hospital, they had waded through the piles of trash covering the front walk and mother had forced the door open, pushing back the trash piled up inside against the door. Inside the house was piled high with stuff; stuff of every conceivable type – furniture, stacks of newspapers, cardboard boxes, and piles of clothes. But mostly the house was full of trash bags of every available color, brown, white, black and green, piled floor to ceiling, all stuffed full.

What is all this stuff? What is in all the bags? Christine had asked.

Nothing, mother had said. Never mind all that—I need to show you to your room.

Carefully they had threaded their way through rooms piled high with trash bags and had come to the house's staircase.

Up, mother had said. Go up.

Christine had gone up and mother had showed her a room that was clear of all the stuff in the rest of the house. It was a beautiful room with a big brand new La-z-Boy set in the far corner, a pink and white dresser and vanity against the wall, and a powder blue bed, and brightly painted yellow walls, and a small window at the far end.

This is your bedroom Christine, mother had said.

This room? This is for me?

Yes—and look—

Mother had opened a narrow door in the side wall of the bedroom and there in another room was a full bathroom with tub sink toilet and beautiful rich red and burgundy colors. Mother had picked up Christine's bag and had put it on the bed with a pat.

Here. I'll go now—you unpack. We'll eat down at Blondie's tonight - to celebrate that you are finally home again.

We are going to eat at Blondie's?

Yes, that right. Blondie's is a little restaurant downtown that you loved when you were just a child.

Suddenly the thought that she was no longer a child frightened Christine and goosebumps swarmed over her. When mother had left the room, Christine had sat in the bright lit yellow room on the edge of her light blue bed. Then she closed her eyes and walked down the winding path between the sunny green lawns and the great lovely trees in the garden that she shared with Leandra.

Leandra, she had called out. You told me that I'd come home. But now what do I do?

Unpack your bags, Leandra had said. You are finally home again.

Christine had unpacked and Leandra had showed her how to hang her clothes in the small closet and how to go into the bathroom and how to shower and get all cleaned up and how to brush down her wet hair. Everything that Leandra showed her were things that Christine would have known had she been out living a life since she was ten instead of being locked up in her own garden of paradise in her mind. Still, she would have been lost if it wasn't for Leandra but Leandra showed her everything; and soon mother showed her some things too.

As the first few days later passed, she had sat with her Mother in their cluttered kitchen piled high with bags of garbage, and in the smell. After a few days Christine had noticed that the other houses on the block did not have garbage piled in the yard like hers and she noticed that the other houses were bright and cheery and inviting whereas hers was overgrown with brushes and the many trees stalking her house shadowed it with gloom. She also noticed that the trash stank two houses away and it was on that day that she got her mother into the kitchen with her and asked,

What should I do for a living Mom? How will I make money?

Oh, the lord will provide, her mother had answered.

But Leandra had already told Christine a sure way to make money.

It was then that the Johns started coming to the house. Christine had picked up her first John outside Blondie's one night after she had finished eating alone. Mother had not been feeling well enough to go out eating. Mother often didn't feel like eating and Leandra had gotten up behind Christine and whispered lightly into her ear.

You've got something men want, Christine. God gave it to you. Men want to fuck. Yes, you know that word. Fuck. It's not just in New York and places like that there are lonely men who need a fuck. There's plenty right here in Nebraska too. Men are the same everyplace—

But I—

Never mind but. You're obliged to use what God gave you. Look. There's a man. You got what he wants. Go on. Ask him—

Leandra lightly ran her finger down Christine's spine and it felt good, so good—she urged her toward a man standing at the bus stop out front.

Him, smiled Leandra. Go on. You'll see. Ask him.

So she went up to the man with Leandra, and asked him.

Hi there, she said—looking for a good time?

What?

I said do you want a good time? I can give you a good time. If you want a good time, come with me. If not, just say so.

He had looked her up and down.

Oh—he had said. I don't know.

Tell him one hundred bucks. At your place, Leandra had whispered in her hear.

One hundred dollars for a night at my place, she said, with not a bit of nervousness in her voice.

Stand closer, Leandra suggested.

She had stood closer.

When the man had said yes, she smiled and they got in the car together and she drove him back to her home. Thelma had been in the kitchen when the loud muffler of the Lincoln had come up outside. Christine had come in with the man.

Mom, Christine had said. This is—what's your name?

Lewis. Just Lewis.

Thelma had said Hello, Lewis.

And Lewis and Christine spent the entire night upstairs in her bed. All night Leandra showed Christine things that she already knew how to do. The next morning Christine drove Lewis back to Blondie's and she had her first steady customer. Back home, she showed Mother the hundred dollars. Mother looked deeply into her daughter's eyes.

Give me fifty of that, we need groceries.

And she turned away, the money crushed in her hand. The money was all that mattered.

After Lewis, Leandra showed Christine how to get more Johns. And she did. The money came in easy. Three years passed this way until one day Thelma cornered Christine in the upstairs hall with a question.

Are you going to get a real job? she asked.

This is a real job, said Christine, handing over her two hundred dollars.

Thelma said nothing going back down the stairs with the money again tightly bundled in her fist. Christine returned to her bedroom to where Leandra was. Leandra was sitting on the edge of the bed facing the vanity mirror. She was beautiful.

I will always show you what to do, breathed Leandra, smiling from the mirror into Christine's face. I will show you everything you need to know to do, as I always have. Trust me.

As they had for several years now, the two walked the winding pebbled path between the green lawns with the spreading beautiful trees above and the springtime light and air, just as they had at the hospital.

See how easy life can be, said Leandra—when you have somebody like me who knows how things are.

How did you get to know so much—what's your secret? Christine asked.

Use what God gave you—that's all—like that—there!

The very next morning Thelma came up, waving a notice from the Deshler zoning office in Christine's face.

I don't know what I'm going to do, cried her mother, waving the notice desperately back and forth. I wish to God Martin was here, he'd have know what to do.

Mom, said Christine, Clean the damned place up, that will help.

I—I can't do that.

Why not?

I can't do it without Martin.

Tears rolled down her cheeks as she repeated, I need Martin to tell me what to do.

Christine pointed to a corner of the living room and narrowed her eyes.

There, she said—Martin's there.

A tall thin man in glasses stood waist-deep in the garbage.

I don't see anyone, said Thelma.

I do—Martin, said Christine to the man—will you help us today?

Don't mock me Christine, snapped the old woman—it's wrong—stop it, just stop it!

She clapped her hands over her ears as Martin said that he would, if he could. But, he couldn't.

But dead people can do things, Christine protested. I know that. I know that because—

Christine, cried her mother. Stop it! Stop saying that, stop talking like that—snap out of it!

As she slapped Christine across the face, Martin melted back into the garbage. Christine didn't care that she'd just been slapped in the face. Instead she looked at Mother with great soft eyes and reached her arms out to her.

Mom, she said—Mom, come here.

Thelma came towards her and they embraced in the kitchen surrounded by the bags of trash. Christine whispered into her mother's ear.

Mom, we'll hire somebody—we'll get somebody to clean the place out——how much time does the notice say we have?

We have two weeks, and then an inspector will come and decide if we can live here anymore.

Christine's face paled—can't live here anymore—can't live here anymore—the words echoed in Christine's head. She let go of the old woman.

Mom, where's your phone book?

Oh I don't know. Why?

I'm going to see who can come to clean out this house. What is it they say? Take the bull by the horns, is what they say; yes, we got to take the damned bull by the horns! Now where's the damned phone book? Tell me now! Where?

I don't know—it's buried somewhere. I never call anybody anyway.

Well we're going to make a call right now – we don't have any time. Which room is it in? I swear to God, I will tear this house apart to find it—how can you not know where your damned phone is?

I don't know, said Thelma, sinking into her unburied chair in the kitchen and wringing her liverspotted hands.

We can't clean up, she sobbed—we can't. Not without Martin.

Then what are we going to do, Mom?

The old woman bent forward and continued to sob as Christine pulled trash bags aside in a desperate search for a phone book, any phone book—her bright room upstairs that she shared with Leandra and her Johns was at stake—her one clean, uncluttered, bright cheery room, that had welcomed her back from the hospital, would be gone. The door to the pebbled road between the wide lawns would be taken from her and Leandra. And the house would collapse in onto itself under the weight of all the trash—the house, the room; it would all be gone into a gaping hole in the ground.

What the hell are we going to do Mom? she shouted as she dug.

We've got to do something.

What the hell will we do?

2 – Reduplicative Paramnesia

LEWIS WAS HER FIRST AND STEADIEST JOHN. HE PAID EXTRA FOR HER to come get him and bring him to her house and her wide comfortable bed where they would lie together day after day, and sit and talk for hours afterwards. Because he listened, Christine liked talking to Lewis. He would sit on the chair across the room, his legs crossed, smoking a cigarette, nodding at everything she said. It was like having a husband—after they were through in bed, that is. He sat in the chair with his shirt off looking at her, his bushy grey hair lit by the soft light that came through the thin pull-down shade in front of the wide window behind him. The smoke of the cigarette snaked around his head and shone lightly in the haze.

So what's new with you? He said smiling broadly. Still being stalked by the president?

How?—Yeah, you know it, she said. Ever since I've known you.

What do you mean? Ever since you've known me?

Every since I knew you I started imagining that I've been fucking the president.

I didn't know you were imagining that, he said, smiling. A wide gap showed between his two top teeth. Tell me about it. He took a drag.

I imagine that you're the president, she said. Simple. That's it. I told you this before—

He leaned back smiling even more broadly.

I know but I like to see you sitting there naked telling me about it. Do you think Mr. President is good in bed? Is it because he's powerful? Like me?

Right—at least as powerful as you Lewis, she said. Hey listen, I have a question now.

What?

What do you do for a living Lewis? I'm surprised you haven't told me.

I'm a pipefitter. I work over in Hebron.

A pipefitter?—what does that mean?

He sat up, cleared his throat, and spoke as though reading from a book.

Pipefitters lay, install, assemble, fabricate, maintain, repair and troubleshoot mechanical piping systems carrying fuel, chemicals, water, steam and air in heating, cooling, lubricating and various other process piping systems, he said quickly. How do you like that? That's what I had to memorize in vocational school, and I still remember it to this day.

You went to school for that? she said.

You bet.

I never went to school, she said.

No?

No. The good Lord gave me all that I need to do my job.

He cracked a grin—I can see that, he said.

She sat up taller on the bed and tucked her legs beneath her.

Good. I'm glad you can see that. You know I really should get dressed now.

Why? You should go out like this, you look fine just the way you are.

Very funny.

She rose and went over to a chair in the corner and started getting dressed from clothes tossed over it. She smelled his smoke—as she sat on the bed, her back to him and slid on her stockings. As she dressed, she asked him more questions.

Where do you work? Do you have your own business or what?

I work at the acid plant—American Solvents—like I said, over in Hebron.

The pay must be pretty good for you to be able to afford me.

The pay is all right. I do part-time work too—for a plumbing contractor in Neville.

Neville? I've been to Neville.

Yeah? Nice town.

Yeah it's nice. So is that where you tell your wife you are when you're here with me—working in Neville?

Yes, that's what I do.

Don't you feel bad lying to your wife? Aren't you ever afraid that you'll get caught? she said as she pulled on her jeans and looked him straight in the eye.

No I'm not afraid. My wife—I hate to say it—she's pretty stupid.

Hey, she said, straightening and fastening her belt—that's not a nice thing to say.

Well, I'm not the one who says it, she admits it herself. Always says that she might not be the brightest bulb in the world, but—

But what?

But whatever, you know—whatever we're talking about.

Doesn't she notice the money you spend here?

Nope, he said, shifting his cigarette from one hand to the other. I handle the money.

She leaned over and pulled on a slipper, looking up at him and smiling.

You're a bastard, you know that, Lewis?

Yeah I know that, he smiled. He dragged on the cigarette, exhaled, and the smoke became a ring around his head and then drifted up above. But my wife doesn't give me what you do.

I appreciate that, she said, pulling on the other slipper, her hair hanging down.

Can't, or won't? she asked, as she leaned back, straightening and smoothing her hair.

I suppose a little of both.

Okay, she said—now the ugly business part—give here, she said, putting out her hand. For you, today—one hundred and fifty dollars.

He reached for his wallet.

Why the discount? he said, fumbling with the cigarette in his hand.

I like you Lewis, she said. I'm realizing that it's almost as much of a pleasure for me as it is for you.

It is? Almost? he said—I thought I was better than that—

Perfection is God's alone, Lewis.

He stubbed out his butt in the big green ashtray sitting on the corner of the pink dresser and sat forward.

Well—I guess you ought to take me back now. Enough fun for one night, don't you agree?

No not now, Lewis. Light up another. Sit awhile. I like talking to you—

Okay, he said, pulling out another cigarette from his top pocket. I like talking to you too.

She didn't tell him that now with the night pressing in all around the house, the house now sat in the middle of a jungle, in the deepest darkest forbidden part. There were no ways in or out—no roads in or out. And because she failed to tell him this, he also didn't know that the jungle that pressed in all around the house every night was crawling with deadly creatures. He didn't know that the only choice for him now was to stay the night, and they could try to hack their way out of the hellish mass of vegetation, vermin and predators in the morning, when the light would have started coming up. In a night like this, the jungle, thick leaved and glistening green, was a death trap, and evil creatures were out hunting.

Say Lewis—how about you stay the night, she said.

Hmm, said Lewis, having lit his cigarette. Does that increase the price?

Why? Are you assuming that we will do something more tonight?

Yes, I guess I am assuming that.

He grinned and took a long drag and blew it out.

Fifty dollars more for the rest of the night, she said—Do you have that much?

I do, you know I do.

He handed over the whole two hundred dollars after fumbling with his wallet once more. He smoked hard—long and fast and hard—just like he was in bed. His smoke layered in the room. But at least they were safe from the jungle, locked inside, Christine thought to herself.

Give me a minute, said Christine—I just got to go tell my mom you're staying the night.

He smiled and took a drag. She went out the door and stumbled through the waist-deep garbage. Christine struggled down the stairs and across the living room kicking garbage bags aside that had fallen from the piles on each side blocking the pathway through, and she went into the kitchen. Thelma was there in a grey robe with her hair in curlers, draped over the chair with her TV flickering in black and white atop the trash.

Mom, said Christine, shuffling through the trash steadying the piles on either side of her—Mom, Lewis is staying the night, please stay out of my bedroom while he's here.

You know I don't like that, said Thelma. You know it's wrong to let them stay the night.

Puts money in our pockets Mom. We'll always have money.

The old woman looked up with her watery blue eyes, raised eyebrows, and grim mouth set. Christine didn't know where they really were—on the surface of the moon, on its dark side, in the sub zero temperatures, with no way back. Leandra stood next to mother, nodding, pointing to the stairs and wagging her finger for Christine to go back up and to get back to work with Lewis. Upstairs, the house was surrounded by jungle; downstairs, it set on the plains of the moon. Thank God mother had no idea where they really were—she'd have gone mad with the realization that there was no way out. Only Christine and Leandra could stand knowing the truth. Not until morning would it be safe to go outside—back into the neighborhood, across the yard and down the street into town. Christine would have gotten a good night's sleep by then—good enough to make the difference. But she was tired now—she was someplace else.

Good night Mom. I'm going upstairs.

Okay. Night night, my dear. Take care of yourself, alright?

Christine left Thelma staring at her television and went back out along the path between the mounds of garbage bags with Leandra by her side.

You're doing the right thing, said Leandra—it's deadly out there. If you leave, you'll die either way.

Yes, whispered Christine—I just hope that mother or Lewis doesn't look out the window to see where they really are—they wouldn't be able to understand it—I don't know what they would do about it.

Never mind that, said Leandra—never mind if they look out. It's too dark for them to see. Right now, you need to go satisfy Lewis. He paid you the extra money so that you would satisfy him. And besides, you like him. You've even said that having sex with him is like having sex with the president.

Yes I do—

They both went back up to the bedroom and Christine set about satisfying Lewis. Leandra sat watching from a corner chair. When it was all over Lewis lay there sleeping in the dark of the room while Leandra and Christine sat at opposite ends of the rowboat. The sea heaved about them and the night's dark stretched all around, closing in on them. Lewis lay between them on the center seat, his eyes lolling open.

That was good, he told Christine as he dipped his hand over the side of the rowboat and into the water —and the water is so cold—

Christine cautioned him; don't put your hand in the water you don't know what's in there.

What do you mean?

What I said—there are creatures in the water—

Leandra stopped rowing and held out a hand toward Christine.

Don't talk Christine—he is asleep you might wake him.

But he's sitting right here—he spoke to me—

His words, what he says, is all meaningless.

Christine what do you mean, said Lewis.

Ignore him, said Leandra.

Christine turned her head out toward the dark, cold, damp sea night. The stars arched overhead and the moon set full just above the horizon, its light glinting off the tossing swells.

Aren't the stars beautiful? asked Leandra.

Yes they are.

But I'm confused, said Christine.

Why?

We were just in the jungle, and now we are at sea.

What are you talking about, said Lewis—where are we?

Christine looked down into the bottom of the boat.

This is hard, she told Leandra—should we get rid of him?

Get rid of me? Why would you want to get rid of me—you were the one that said I should stay overnight.

Yes, I think we should, said Leandra—and she reached out and pushed Lewis off the seat and into the water. He hung on to the side of the boat and Leandra used her paddle to smash at his hands until he let go and he disappeared into the dark waters with barely a struggle.

Why did you do that? asked Christine.

He'll be all right—he'll be asleep in your bed when you get back.

But he was talking to me—

No more. He's asleep in your bed, right next to you.

But we are on the sea!

The sea is just as good a place as any. They drifted a while until Leandra leaned over on an elbow and spoke.

You know you're doing all right for yourself. You know that, don't you?

Yes I suppose so.

Considering how long you were in that hospital in the state that you were in—you're doing really well.

I owe it to my mother. She stuck by me. She came and sat with me whenever she could —every night sometimes. She worked in the dress factory all day and then came to be with me all night. She talked to me when I couldn't talk with anyone else. But we did manage to talk. We talked about all kinds of things—this is right before I met you. She also kept my room ready for me to come home. And when I got home she brought me clothes and food.

But it was her fault you were in the hospital to begin with.

Christine looked up at the dome of stars and the moon.

It wasn't her fault, mother was like she was, said Christine.

What about the way she is now—is the way she is now her fault?

It was a shock losing Daddy.

Letting the house go to stink—isn't that her fault?

But my room is fine. When I'm in my room the rest of the house isn't there. Other places are there. The jungle. The moon. The sea. As the sun came around the edges of the shades, the dome of stars and the moon dissolved and the bed formed and the room returned with Lewis in the bed, on his side facing away from Christine, rumpled with a sheet over him, sound asleep. Christine looked up at the ceiling—so white, so pure, so smooth, so unlike the rest of the house. As the jungle moon and sea were fading—morning came brighter around the shade. Morning, and Lewis—God, Lewis had to get to work now, fast. It's a workday for this pipefitter—this one that works at the acid plant out in Hebron. He had to get there on time on time. Lewis! she said loudly, shaking his shoulder. Lewis!

He started.

Christine, he oozed, rolling over. Christine—

Don't you have to be at work this morning Lewis? What time do you have to be at work?

Oh. I'm going to call in sick today. I—I'm too tired to work. You wear me out—but tell me. How was the president last night?

She cracked a grin.

Oh. He was great—say tell you what if you're not going to work maybe we could go out for breakfast. I'll let you pay.

You'll let me pay.

Yeah. I'll give you the honor. Hey listen.

What, he said, rising and reaching for his clothes draped over the chair back by the bed.

What about your wife? It just occurred to me—where does your wife think you were all night? You never called her—

Oh Christ! he snapped, striking himself in the forehead with the heel of his hand. I forgot to call her.

What will you tell her? How could you have forgotten to call her?

Christ I don't know. I wasn't thinking. I can't go to breakfast with you Christine. I need to go home. I have to tell her something. Maybe I can tell her that I broke down.

Broke down?

Yeah.

But you have a cell phone. She'll wonder why you didn't call her on the cell phone.

He pulled up his pants and threw on his shirt and sat heavily on the bed.

Christ I really fucked up this time, he said. I—I just got to face it. I'll tell her I was out drinking all night. That's all. That's the only story I can tell her. She will be damned pissed!

Have you ever been out drinking all night before?

Yeah—years ago when I had a problem.

Problem?

Yah. I had a drinking problem—anyway Christine—I'm ready for you to drive me to my car okay? We have got to go right now.

Well—I think I probably should get dressed first—

Well hurry up.

Why don't you call her now—and tell her that the contractor called you and there was an emergency job at another one of the plants that took all night—or at your own plant—the acid works in Hebron—you can say they called you in to handle an emergency there.

But why didn't I call last night?

Christine shrugged.

No time. As a matter of fact tell her you still need to stay at the plant for a few hours. That way you and I can still go to breakfast.

She smiled.

That's the answer, she said. Okay?

There was one time a few years back where we had to work all night at the factory because there was a big leak.

Yeah—tell her that—go on. Call her from here.

He sank into the chair by the window and lit up a cigarette before pulling out his cell phone and dialing. Lewis' face was as white as a sheet, as he sat quietly for a while, then his wife answered.

Allie? It's me—please forgive me for not calling before now—we had a big emergency at the plant—they called me in—I didn't have time to call you—I'm so so sorry if I worried you.

He fell silent with the phone pressed to his ear. Christine could hear his wife's voice in the phone across the room.

I—I couldn't call—we were in a room with solvents—flammable—you can't use a cell phone in there, it was an emergency. They called me, called me late—I didn't want to wake you—

She yelled.

No, he said—no I'm not lying. Allie, please.

He pulled the phone down from his ear.

God damn it, he said—she hung up on me. Says I'm lying. Says she wants my boss at the acid works to call and tell her it's true.

So pay him.

What?

He's a man. Men are all alike. He'll cover for you—for a few bucks.

I—I don't think I can do that. Only a real scumbag would do that.

A scumbag with guts. Okay, she said—come on I'll drive us to breakfast.

No I need to go home.

Are you sure?

Yes. I need to go home and make it right.

She laughed.

Hey—just have Mr. President throw her on the bed. She'll believe you.

Yeah right.

Right.

As they went out the door, Christine turned back and winked into her vanity mirror.

3 – Mount Everest I

I DON'T KNOW IF I'M GOING TO GO TO CHRISTINE'S ANY MORE. NEVER mind that I had the biggest fight with Allie when I got home. She said she was going to leave me. She said she wanted my boss to call her. I don't know where that will lead, but after two days, at least she's speaking to me again. I can't pay my boss to call her. I just won't. This thing with Allie will blow over. It isn't the first time I stayed out all night and didn't call. It used to happen a lot when I'd go on a bender. I think I'll just own up and say I was on a bender. Allie at least will understand that. If she ever knew about Christine, though—watch out!

Christine is nice enough mostly but that house she lives in looks like it's sagging in on itself and it will fall in any minute, like that TV show 'Hoarders'? That's Christine's mom—it's just as bad, if not worse, than anything I've seen on the TV. I can't hardly make it to Christine's room—it's all dark and I stumble over all the loose trash up along the stairs, but once I'm in her room, watch out! It's beautiful. Just like her. She's worth every dollar—every damned dollar. But she's crazy goose too—crazy crazy goose. Like the one night she went off on Mount Everest—that was spooky. We were in the room nice—I was smoking in the chair—I mean she's got a chair that's heaven to sit in, it's so comfortable—I could sleep

forever in that damned chair. La-Z-Boy or something I think—
but anyway. She's on the bed looking into the vanity mirror like
she does, and she starts—starts talking like there's somebody else
there. It's like I'm not there anymore; like there's somebody on
the other side of the mirror. I had taken a few of her pills so I sat
calm—she's always got pills around—don't know where she gets
'em—but I sat calm and watched and listened and smoked and it
was something to watch.

It's like I'm not here now, you know—it's like I'm on Everest.

Everest? I said—you meant the big mountain?

Yes, yes—Everest is there right now—Everest is there and we are
there too—everyplace is there and here too. We're everyplace—

She went on a while like this, with that glassy look in her eyes
getting deeper the longer she talked into the mirror, it seemed like
hours; and by then I had gotten so spooked that I almost ran—but
the pills were good and strong and so I sat tight smoking.

—we can't leave the house, she said—it's too cold out there and
there's a hell of a drop—drop to the bottom. All the way down,
you know? All the way down—

She got quiet then, and turned smiling to me, and her eyes
looked okay again, but it was then that she asked me to stay the
night. When I said that I didn't have enough money she became
very nervous and glanced into the mirror and then turned to me.

I tell you what, she said—you're a regular—you can stay and
it'll be on the house.

I looked down from the smile, then into her eyes again.

No, I really need to get home, I told her—and she got all
scared-looking. She crossed her arms on her chest and closed her
eyes.

Please, please—you need to stay. Please just one time. This time.

So I gave in again, just like I did last night. But I wondered what all the talk about Mount Everest was about—so I asked her about Mount Everest, and she got all wide-eyed and surprised.

Was I talking out loud about Mount Everest? Silly me! she said, and she laughed it off, sitting there half naked on the bed.

No really, I said—who were you talking to in the mirror?

Nobody.

But then, she started talking to me about Mount Everest—and everything she said to me was spooky—really, really spooky. I got ready by chewing onto another pill, hunkering down into the chair and dragging on my smoke while I grabbed onto the chair arms and listened. Her voice was like the wind blowing—she was like a preacher as she held out her hands, her palms facing upwards, pointing to a distant peak above her bed.

Look now, there—right now, right there—the tip of Mount Everest—windblown and icy. The wind is blowing—the wind is always blowing. Can you feel it? she asked me. That's where we are right now—atop the peak of Mount Everest. This room is up high, too high to leave—can you feel the air? The air is thin. If you go out the door you will die. You die. Go on, try—just go on. Go on and try—you'll die from the frozen wind and the thin air, your body tumbling thousands of feet below, and landing, where? Who knows how far you'll fall, and where?

I said nothing, I just looked at her because what do you say when somebody is talking this way? Besides I was full of the pills and I thought that maybe she wasn't really saying anything—maybe it was just the pills mouthing those words in her about Mount Everest. Still she went on.

Have you ever heard of George Mallory? Mallory ring a bell?

No, I replied.

He fell off Everest in 1921 and his body wasn't found until 1999. Isn't that amazing?

I nodded and pulled on a drag as she went on.

I saw it in the newspaper in the hospital, she said. I always read the newspapers in the hospital. There isn't much else to do in the hospital. You know.

What were you in the hospital for?

It really—well, it kind of was a hospital I suppose—it was a mental institution, a nut house—I was in the nut house for twenty years. I read about George Mallory who had lain there on Mount Everest dead for seventy eight years with all the wind and cold and snow and ice whipping all around his body. You know?

I nodded, she coughed, then went on.

I thought I was a lot like him you know, just laying there as good as dead in the nut house the only difference being that in there there's heating in the winter and it doesn't snow rain and freeze on you—and it's hot in the summer though I bet it was hot in the summer on George Mallory where he lay there flat on his face all those years unmoving—isn't it amazing how something can lie in the same place, not moving, for longer than we've been alive?

Yes it is—

I saw an actual picture of him on the computer where they found him and all—he was on his stomach and his head was buried in the loose stones, his back and arm were bare and his buttocks were sticking out there—his clothes had rotted off him—and there were holes in his buttocks—big holes in his ass cheeks—you could see they were black as night.

She stopped, smiled slightly, and I knew she was finished. I just dragged on my cigarette and nodded—yes, it was truly amazing how that poor guy had laid there for seventy eight years—but a question that had sat in my mind while she was talking suddenly came out.

Why were you in the nut house, Christine?

Her face did not change and she did not seem surprised.

I was crazy, she said.

Crazy?

Yes. I just wasn't myself, I wasn't myself—I suppose, so yes, I was crazy.

But crazy means so many different things, I protested—we're all crazy at times, like how I was crazy that night when I forgot to call Allie and then I feel terrible about it in my head? Where was my head? I always called Allie before I don't know—

I paused to catch my breath.

Don't know what? she asked—what don't you know?

Okay, I'll say it right out--there's something about you, Christine that makes me forget things. Nothing bad, you understand, please don't think that. But there's something.

Something? Like what?

Like how you went on and on about Mount Everest and this guy Mallory—

She pushed up her hand.

Oh, yes, Mallory. Poor Mallory. He was just climbing along and then, POW, down he goes—what must it be like to fall that far? And then to just lay there for seventy eight years. Actually it was longer because the people that found him didn't bring him down—they did an Anglican service over him and then piled stones on top of him and left him there—in what they call a cairn burial.

Cairn burial?

Yes. Cairn burial. I read in a book that a cairn burial is just a pile of stones, so my question is what keeps them from falling all apart if they don't cement the stones in and they just stack them on top of each other, Mallory might be laying right there right now the way he did for seventy eight years all uncovered. And what if the cairn breaks down and the stones all scatter, so that he'll be lying there for another seventy eight years. What do you think of that? Huh?

I suppose that's possible, I said, with smoke coming out my mouth and nose when I said that because I had just taken a big drag off my cigarette. As I looked at her I saw that her eyes were on fire. Seeing this made me want to leave. I stubbed out my cigarette in the glass ashtray on the vanity and started to rise.

Well, Christine, that's enough talk of old mummified corpses lying on mountains—do you think you could drive me now back to the acid works?

I always left my car down at the acid works, before I met Christine at Blondie's—that way if somebody sees my car they'll think I'm working because if they saw my car at Christine's, they'd know. Oh yah, everybody knows Christine is a whore, but many don't know how crazy she is; like last night how she answered me.

No, we can't get down, we're atop Mount Everest, you need to stay the night before we can get down. It's too cold outside, the wind will die in fifteen minutes. I want you to stay with me.

Well I figured since I didn't have to pay extra, why not. I had the brains this time to call Allie and tell her that I was pulling another double shift at the acid works and wouldn't be home until morning and all she asked was whether I was getting paid double time and I told her yes from Christine's comfy chair with Christine looking back at me, smiling from where she lay naked, one leg draped over the side of her bed and when I hung up she called me over.

Lewis, said Christine, stretching out her arms—come on, I'm ready, let's get to it.

Okay, no problem. None at all—

So I came to her and we went to it for a while but I wasn't very good because of the pills that I had taken before but she was fine—and that went on for about an hour and then we both went to sleep in her bed. When I woke up it was about three in the morning and Christine was sitting up in her bed talking to herself like she was two people and I lay my head onto the pillow and I listened, wondering what did this mean now, was she really still a nut. I listened as she was talking about the stars and the moon and how wonderful they all were overhead, which was silly because we were in the dark of her bedroom and then she put on another voice and said something about yes they are so beautiful out here in the middle of the sea, and I thought, What the hell is she talking about? First it was all about Mallory and his Mount Everest and now it was about the stars, the moon and the sea and she was in a boat. When she talked it made the bed feel like it was moving like a boat floating in the water would move. She looked at me then.

Look, Lewis—look at all the sparkles from the moon dancing over the water—

I looked, and I just saw the wall and the floor. Actually it was really dark so I wasn't seeing either the wall or the floor, but I knew that they were there. I knew we weren't out in a boat at sea, we couldn't have been. While I searched over the edge of the bed, the two of them kept on talking—I mean, Christine talking in her two voices and after a while I drifted back to sleep. The next morning she took me down to breakfast in her Mother's old Lincoln.

You know, my Mom is pretty funny, she said as the car rolled down to town.

Oh yeah? What is so funny about your mother?

When I got out of the hospital I had wanted to learn how to drive a car—and Mom told me I needed something called a license, and I just looked at her and said What for? A license has nothing to do with driving a car, a license is just a little card, it doesn't help you to drive the car. And so I told Mom I don't need no damned license—and I never got one—

She laughed then as we went over a bump, then went on.

This really burns Mom up, that I drive this big old car with no license—but really. Who needs one? You know?

Crazy talk, more crazy talk from Christine. Since she seemed in such a good mood, laughing out loud and all, I thought I'd ask her another question.

Who were you talking to in the middle of the night last night? I asked.

Oh—nobody, she said. We—we were just lucky the room had come down from Mount Everest during the night. You know what I mean Lewis? We are damned lucky.

Come down from Mount Everest? What? I was totally confused.

When she talks like that it almost makes me think I might not go back to her—though she's just so damned good at what she does. But things do get odd, very odd. Like last night. I woke up and heard her sitting up at the foot of the bed, naked, cross-legged, having a conversation with herself. With herself! I sat up.

What are you talking about Christine? I said. Who are you talking to? Who's here with us?

Shut up, she said—you're supposed to be asleep, so go back to sleep—and then she just kept on talking to herself.

But there's no one there—here, here—come by me—

No! I am busy! she snapped, and just went on softly talking into the empty dark. I'll admit I was annoyed.

Christine! Stop it! There's nothing there! Let's get real—

She leapt up and turned around and kicked out at me and knocked me off the bed onto the floor—and I tried to pull myself up from falling and she kicked at my hands and I fell over onto the floor. I was scared—but she went on talking.

My mother was the one who got me through being in the hospital so long, damn you, you had nothing to do with it so keep quiet—

Crazy, it was just crazy—so I just laid on the floor and after a while of yelling at me she got quiet; I peered up over the edge of the bed and she was naked, stretched out on the bed asleep and I got back in the bed next to her and then I too fell back asleep in her dark room. Once asleep, I had a dream the likes of which I couldn't believe. I think it probably came from the weird woman in the bed next to me. I dreamt that eight-foot tall aliens had come down and they had big, bald heads with ugly looks on their faces and they wore long robes. They looked like the aliens in the Twilight Zone story about the ones who came with a book the title of which was "To Serve Man." But instead of carrying a book, these aliens in my dream each held a weapon and they said to me, succumb to us or face the wrath of our weapons—and nobody wanted to succumb to them so they pushed buttons on their weapons and their guns unwound like they were wrapped with wire and there was something inside made of leather rolled up and they pointed it at you and it unrolled at you and it was the Holy Bible—just a regular Holy Bible with gold leaf lettering and a black leather cover. They held the book out and they said, Now you must follow this—you have no choice—we knew you would not succumb to us otherwise so we had to resort to these most powerful weapons. Then they slapped the bibles into our hands and we turned and walked away and we started to read it—and this 'good book', as they called it, ended up changing the world just like they said it would. The dream didn't have anything to do with Christine, at least not directly, but her weird talking to herself probably put me in the mood where I was dreaming of those aliens. Still I don't know if I'll go back but something in me cares about her no matter how weird she is, about mummified bodies on mountain tops and boats in the middle of the night and the room being squat right on top of Mount Everest and that's why we couldn't leave for the night. It's just that she is so damned good at what she does, so damned good.

Once, I even asked her, Christine where did you learn to do the things you do.

What do you mean?

The things you do with me in bed?

And she just laughed and looked in her vanity mirror and laughed and laughed and it was like she was laughing with her reflection in the mirror, like her reflection was a different person. Another time when I had the pills in me, I asked again after that time that we dove into the bed and she did me all over one time more.

Damn she was good. I take back what I said about not knowing if I'll go back to be with her. Of course I'll go back to Christine. Yes I will, you bet I will! She's got what it takes. But now, when I get home to Allie I want to be extra nice to her after what I've done. I'll take her dancing and I'll hold her close and try not to imagine that she's Christine. Besides, there's no harm done in that a body is a body in the dark with your eyes closed after all. I can just keep everything that happened to me with Christine inside and Allie will never know about it. She'll just enjoy the dance, no matter what; hot bodies pressed together like that is all, and one body is just as good as another body, isn't it? For sex, I mean. Just for sex.

4 – Deshler Borough Hall

I'm sorry but Mister Barber is not here. He went down to Jefferson County today to handle a few things. What is the problem? I see that you have one of our notices there, is that what it is all about? How can I help you?

The watery-eyed woman grimaced through the window separating them. She had spoken through the holes in the window and she sat there with a grin, her hands set on the shelf before her with a pen in her hand and her eyeglasses chained to her ears with golden chains that swung back and forth when she talked. The sign above her office window said Deshler Borough Code Enforcement. To Christine, it seemed that this was the right place because Mister Barber had signed the notice and the woman nodded when Christine had said Mister Barber and so Christine let out the problem all at once, there down at the Borough Hall.

My mother got this notice on her door that says that she has two weeks to clean out her house and her yard before this Mister Barber is going to come down and do an inspection. I want to put in for an extension on that inspection. We need more than two weeks time to clean her place up. Also I understand there have been complaints?

Yes, said the woman, looking down into a binder she had brought to the window. There have been a total of—thirty six complaints. Your name is Zidar, right?

Yes, yes—but who did the complaining?

I can't tell you that Miss. That will come out in court if this comes to that.

In court?

Yes, in court. If we decide to evict you and you appeal, you'll have to do so at the county court house in Hebron.

If you decide to evict us? What do you mean, evict us?

Yes. Evict is what I said. You've gotten health code violations and thirty six complaints—listen, the simplest and best thing for you to do is to simply clean your place up and pass the inspection—and your troubles here will be over.

Christine glanced over her shoulder as though listening to a voice and then she looked the woman in the center of her green, thick-rimmed glasses.

I want to talk to Mister Barber's boss.

The woman smiled.

You are talking to her.

Christine was pierced by the sharp look of the woman.

And please what is your name?

Petersen. I'm Mrs. Petersen.

Christine listened to the voice over her shoulder as she jotted down the words Miss Petersen on the notice and looked up and said, Listen, Miss Petersen lets be real, what will it take to make this go away?

Make what go away?

This notice. What will it take to make it go away?

You need to clean your place up—

No I mean how much will it take, Christine said, placing her hand on her silver studded bag. How many dollars?

Miss Petersen's eyebrows rose and she tapped the pencil on the window and said, Now don't you try to bribe me—bribing me is against the law.

Enough dollars will make anything go away, said Christine—let's say—three hundred dollars? How about I pay three hundred dollars and you wipe all this off the records?

I can't wipe it off the records, said Miss Petersen. Everthing's all registered in the system. Your inspection date is what it says on that notice. Have the place cleaned up and be ready. And don't try to bribe me again or I'll call for an officer. Spend the three hundred on a cleanup service. If you're so anxious to use money to make this go away that is the way to do it. Are we clear?

Christine glanced back over her shoulder again and then said to Miss Petersen I want a list of the people who have complained.

I can't give you that. I told you already.

Then I want to speak to your boss.

Mrs. Petersen's eyes rolled inside her green rims, chains swinging.

My boss is the Mayor, and he isn't in. Go to his office though—there'll be a receptionist there and you can make an appointment to see him.

Okay, said Christine—I will do that—but off the record—I mean can I talk off the record without you calling for an officer, as you say?

Depends—but go on.

I will give you five hundred dollars in your hand right here, right now to make this thing go away. You see, my Mom is very feeble. She only has a little pension and this house is all she has. She doesn't have what it takes to clean the place up—there is more involved than just going in there and throwing everything out. A lot of that stuff has value to her. She has to have the time to go through everything. I'll tell you what, push the deadline back by a month, and I'll give you the two hundred dollars, just to push the deadline back a month or you can have the five hundred to make the whole thing go away. You'd be making an old feeble woman feel much better—you'd be doing a good deed. Plus you'd have a pocketful of money. But if course I never said this. I'll deny I ever said it. This is just between me and you. What do you say?

Go talk to the Mayor. And please, none of this bribery talk with him. He'll have you locked up. He's a straight arrow. I'm warning you, miss. Don't you dare.

Christine said nothing, turning away clutching the notice. As she moved away from the window and walked toward the Mayor's office, Leandra spoke softly into her ear.

Every man has his price. What will it be with the mayor? You have to change your tack. You have to tell him that this notice from the city is a mistake that needs to be corrected. You have to tell him that the place is spotless now. You have to tell him that the order was written for somebody else, and not for you. He might ask, How did your name get on it? You tell him that it was a mistake—just one of those crazy mistakes. The place is spotless. They could send someone out there right now to check it, but that won't be necessary, because you are telling him the truth. That is how you talk to a Mayor. Don't talk about bribe money. That Miss Petersen was just a flunky. You can try and bribe a flunky. Like, how much money do you suppose Miss Petersen makes? I'm sure she could use the money. She's probably kicking herself in the ass right now for not taking the bribe—why, five hundred dollars is probably a week's pay for her, and just to lose some silly records. I bet they lose records all the time at this place. And what's with the inspector's name? Mister Barber? Heh—a lower flunky than the flunky Mrs. Petersen that you just talked to. You should stop by that window on the way out and find out when Mister Barber will be in. I bet he'd take three hundred, never mind five, Mister Barber would. Hey you know the name of a person a long long time ago was supposed to describe the trade they were in—like Weaver or Smith or Carpenter. Barber—that's one of those names. I bet he comes from a family of barbers. I funny when you think about all the hair that falls onto the floor all around the barber chair after a haircut and how there's a huge mess to clean up, no wonder he's out inspecting houses for trash. He's got it in his blood, that Mister Barber.

Christine walked on, listening intently.

Christine, I know you're tired, it's rough having all this hanging over your head but you have to knock some sense into that mother of yours and get her to clean the place out. To be the Mayor has got to be a big deal. He's no doubt got a great big head. I wonder, how does he get his big head down the hall and into his office? I bet it's a tight scrape. Tight scrape, tight scrape—get it? But here we are. There's the woman Mrs. Petersen was talking about. Go to it Christine.

In a small room, a small woman sat at a desk under a MAYOR OF DESHLER sign. She was writing fast in a yellow legal pad and when Christine entered, she looked up from under the dome of her blonde hair and through her gold rimmed glasses.

Can I help you?

Yes I need to make an appointment to see the mayor.

She put down her pen.

Regarding?

Christine held up the notice.

Regarding this—my mother got it by mistake and Mrs. Petersen downstairs said I need to see the Mayor to correct it.

But—Mrs. Petersen and Mister Barber handle all these types of things. The Mayor would just tell you to see them.

That's the problem, said Christine, her mouth tightening. They said that they won't help me. They said that I need to see the Mayor but he's not in today, so she told me that I have to make an appointment.

All right, said the small blonde, opening a leather-bound scheduling book on her desk. The Mayor is available tomorrow—in the afternoon—let's see—

While the small woman ran the pen down the schedule Christine glanced back at Leandra and Leandra whispered into Christine's ear. There was a computer on the woman's desk and its screen glowed white.

Christine spoke. Miss, she said.

The woman looked up from the schedule. Yes?

Is that computer hooked into the system where these notices are kept?

Yes, why?

Christine leaned down and spoke softly.

You know, she stage-whispered—the problem is that this notice was a mistake—it shouldn't have been sent out to us. The people downstairs say they can't delete it. They told me that the Mayor's office could delete it. That's why they sent me up here. To tell you to delete it.

They said it was okay to delete it?

Yes they said that, said Christine, looking the small lady straight in the eye.

But that's not true that they can't delete it. Why did they say they couldn't delete it?

They said—well they said they wouldn't delete. There's a long story that I have to tell the mayor about my mother to explain it all, and they wouldn't listen. And so I said, well then let me talk to your boss, and Mrs. Petersen said her boss is the Mayor. So I'm here—sorry if I confused things—it's not that they can't delete it— they just won't is all. Anyway—when is the mayor free tomorrow?

He's free at three, or four. But I'm just going to warn you—if Petersen and Barber won't take it off the books, the Mayor won't either. I know how these things go.

Christine leaned down again, taking a stack of dollar bills out of her purse.

I bet this would get you to delete the notice.

She opened her hand before the woman. She held three one hundred dollar bills.

What? said the woman—you're bribing me?

I never said that—

Oh yes you are. You'd better put that money away and I will try to forget it.

But, it's three hundred dollars? Three hundred dollars is a lot of money for me.

I can see that—and if you don't put it back I'll be forced to call an officer. Here—let me see your notice, what kind of notice is it?

Christine handed the notice over.

The woman squinted into the piece of paper and said, This just says that your house will be inspected in two weeks. Why is it being inspected? Let's see—health hazard, it says. Why don't you just clean up the health hazard instead of coming down here to argue with us? The Mayor won't be able to help you—he won't override the code enforcement folks. What's the health hazard?

My mother has a little trash around the place, that's all, said Christine.

A little trash—you mean like hoarding?

I—I wouldn't go as far as that—but she's an old woman, she 'doesn't understand all this. Can't we just leave her alone until she passes? Then I can clean the place out, right quick.

How old is she?

Sixty-three.

She's not that old. She might live the next thirty years. She should be able to handle this. Is she in good health?

She breathes a little heavy sometimes—asthma—she's got a really bad case of asthma.

Well—cleaning the place up will improve that.

No it won't—the case is chronic. Oh, you don't know how sick she is. This whole notice and inspection thing is killing her and making her asthma worse—I—

As she tried to explain herself, feeling her voice start to rise, a tall man in a natty suit and tie and with slicked back hair approached. He leaned over and spoke to the woman behind the desk.

Mary—is this young lady here to see the mayor?

Yes but the Mayor is out today.

Can I help? said the man. I have nothing important happening at the moment.

He looked at Christine. His eyes were brown, clear and alive. He looked into her.

How can I help you Miss? I'm the deputy mayor. I handle things when the mayor is away—here, let me see that notice. Zidar? Are you related to Thelma Zidar?

Yes, yes, I'm her daughter, said Christine—and she went on and told the man the whole problem. He nodded thoughtfully as she spoke, and the woman behind the desk looked on scowling. Christine handed the man the notice and he scanned it carefully.

Hum, he said slowly—you can just appeal this—what, do you want to have the inspection moved back? So you have more time to clean up? Is this a hoarding situation?

Yes it is, said Christine hesitantly.

You can file an extension—Mary, he said to the woman behind the desk. Give this woman a form to file for an extension—

But look at the notice, it says that this is the final notice—no extensions.

He grinned.

Around here, he said, there's no such thing as a final notice. This woman's mother is sick. We've got to take that into consideration.

But that's already been taken into consideration. It says they've had the date moved back five times.

Never mind that. Give her the form. This is America. We care about people here. He turned and walked back toward his office. The blonde woman gave Christine the form.

Fill out this form and take it back to Miss Petersen. But let me warn you—it will get you nowhere—I don't know why he's saying what he's saying—you've already gotten a final notice there.

Christine looked at the form. It was the same form she'd filed five times before.

Thank you, she said to Mary.

Mary nodded with a scowl.

As they walked away, Leandra came close and said, I wonder what her problem is. It's like they want to throw you out of your own house.

I know. But Mom will like this—this will make Mom feel better—and the deputy mayor said it would work. Did you see his eyes?

Yes.

They were the eyes of an honest man. We're in good hands with him, I can feel it. That Mary doesn't know what she's talking about—come on lets go home tell Mom.

People passing by the in the hall stared at Christine talking to herself, but to them she was just, another nut—another nut, she thought to herself. I know what you're thinking—so think it.

She rushed home to tell Thelma what had happened as she held out the form to her.

Our problems are solved, said Christine—we just need to fill this out.

Nonsense, snapped the old woman. She grabbed the form, crumpled it up and tossed it into the piles of garbage. That's nonsense, she said—they just gave you this form to get rid of you. Our inspection notice said the notice is final—this one is for real and for keeps. They are going to have us outta here within the month—

No, exclaimed Christine—the deputy mayor gave this to me, he was a nice man, he meant what he said, I just know it.

He just wanted you out of there and to leave because you were probably being a pest—like you always are.

I am not a pest! I was just trying to help us! We went down there to help you!

Mother turned towards her, eyes on fire.

We? We went down there? Bullshit! What are you talking about? We went down there? What do you mean we? Are you going crazy again and trying to give me one more thing to worry about?

Christine stood still, holding her breath in with Leandra standing behind her—she could feel that Leandra was close—she felt that Leandra was real.

I was never crazy! shouted Christine.

Yes you were—you had that imaginary friend. Apparently you have her still.

I don't have imaginary friends, I have real friends!

What real friends? No one comes to see you but those Johns you bring in here.

They are also my friends!

That's nonsense, and you know it. Christine why do you talk nonsense? Why can't you just stay in your room and leave me alone?

Crazy? said Christine—How dare you call me crazy? Damn you—look at how you keep this damned house of yours! It's your fault we're getting kicked out—

We're not getting kicked out.

Yes we are, because of this—

Christine swung her arm against a wall of stacked trash bags and the wall fell completely burying Thelma's chair and blocking their way and Thelma stood there shaking, knee-deep in the avalanche of trash and screamed.

Damn you Christine! I ought to throw you out of here. You're nothing but trouble. Look what you've done you damned slut—

This God-damned slut pays all the bills, Mom—the bills—now clean up your shit, all your shit's blocking the way.

You knocked it down, you need to help me.

I don't need to do anything to help you. This house full of trash is yours. I bring the money in. And I am not a slut. I don't enjoy what I do—but like every other God-damned thing I do, I do it for you! You're a bitch. Deep down mom—you are nothing but a crazy hoarder bitch!

Martin wouldn't put up with talk like that—he's here all the time—his spirit is. If he was more than a spirit he would brain you—I know he would, for talking to me like that.

My Father is dead Mom! Get it through your head, my Father is dead!

Stricken, Thelma clutched her breast theatrically and sunk into the pile of trash bags, while Christine, with Leandra, made their way past her and up toward Christine's room.

I hate that woman, muttered Christine.

You do now—but it will pass—

No it won't pass. I really do hate that woman! I hate her, I hate her house and I hate her mess.

Leandra said nothing as they went up the stairs. When Christine reached her bed and threw herself on it, Leandra lay down next to her and her arm came around and Christine was asleep in a place where great, dark shapes strove against each other under the black waters, groaning and grunting and bellowing, but Leandra was there and so she kept her calm. And when the dreams of the night seas was over she rose and went and took a shower and cleaned up to be ready for when another friend would come visit her tonight. Good for five hundred, she muttered to herself. Five hundred dollars for mother, she said as she washed her hands until they were raw and burning with hate.

5 – Capgras Delusion

AT SEVEN O'CLOCK CAME A KNOCK AT THE DOOR. CHRISTINE struggled through the trash and opened the door with some difficulty, pushing against piles of plastic bags. A dark haired portly middle aged man stood there smiling.

Christine! he said. Christine, I'm here—good to see you again. Her face fell.

No, she said. You're not Mr. Tanady. Where is Mr. Tanady? Mr. Tanady's supposed to be here at seven. Who are you?

The man looked around and back and said I'm Mr. Tanady—Ronald Tanady. We have an appointment at seven. I've been here before. What do you mean I'm not Mr. Tanady?

They stood nose to nose at the door. A fly buzzed past, as another buzzed out.

Don't get me wrong, Sir, said Christine—I'll still do you. I don't mind that Ronnie sent someone else in his place. As long as your money's good. But tell me do you know why Ronnie sent you here in his place?

I don't understand.

Never mind, she said, leaning out through the doorway and taking his hand in the midst of the buzzing flies. Come on in. If you got money, I don't care if you're not Ronnie. You do look just like him though. Your disguise is very nice. Are you going to keep the disguise on while we do it? Or are you going to let me see who you really are?

I—I'm not wearing a disguise, he said, stepping over the trash.

Okay. I'll go along with it, she winked. If this is how Ronnie wants it to be—I'm okay with it, too.

Together they moved through the impassible kitchen. Thelma had picked up some of the trash that had fallen during their argument but nowhere near all of it. They got to the stairs, and went up, squeezing past the boxes cluttering the stairs. Unopened deliveries from the Home Shopping Network, boxes full of limited-edition toys, heirloom quality dolls and must-have kitchen helpers and larger boxes with nothing on them to indicate what they held where propped up on every stair—Christine and Mr. Tanady squeezed past all of them to get to the landing where they went to her door, Christine kicking the trash in the hallway aside. She opened the door and switched on the light to her bedroom as they went in. Mr. Tanady sat on the bed and pulled off his shoes. Christine stood over him.

Come on, she said, hands on her hips. Before we go any further, tell me who you really are. Take off the mask.

I—Christine, I'm not wearing a mask—I'm Ronnie—look—look.

He leaned forward and pulled his wallet from his back pocket and opened it to his driver's license. He pulled out the license and handed it to Christine. She stood examining it as he also pulled out his credit cards and handed them over. She looked at the cards, turned them over in her hands, squinted and scrunched up the corner of her mouth and handed the cards back to him.

Well, I suppose if Ronald trusted you enough to carry his wallet and carry all his cards I suppose I can trust you too. I noticed money in there—you know you owe me three hundred for tonight, right? Did Ronald tell you?

As he put away the cards and his wallet he sighed, rolled his eyes and said Yes, Christine—Mr. Tanady told me.

She stood silently eyeing him.

I just wish I knew who you really are, she said softly.

I am Ronald Tanady, he said, raising a hand. But who am I to complain. I've got the money, love—so let's do it.

Together they got undressed and got under the covers in her bed and spent the next two hours busy with Christine's work. She was magnificent. This fake Mr. Tanady's pleasure was secondary. Leandra lay with them for a while, helping Christine. The bed heaved and creaked and at last Christine lay under the sheet and Ronald lay spent over the edge of the bed.

You are wonderful Christine—just like always. I am so happy to have you.

What do you mean just like always? Isn't this your first time?

Oh, yeah, right—I'm not Mr. Tanady. I'm just someone else wearing a mask that he sent in his place. Jeez Christine, believe what you want to.

He reached over and picked up a used condom that had fallen to the floor, knotted it and tossed it in a pink plastic garbage can that matched the rest of her room. Then he lay down next to her atop the sheet. The sheet is between us now, she thought—yes, this was how Ronald always behaved, muttered Christine—amazing how you've got all Ronald's moves down—and your mask—that mask is perfect. Even when we were in the thick of things, the mask stayed on perfectly, she whispered to Leandra. She glanced at his profile as he lit a cigarette in bed, having gotten his smokes and ash tray from the vanity. He even lights up and smokes just like Ronald—how did Mr. Tanady teach him all this? I'll have to ask Tanady the next time I see him. Or should I see him again?

Ask him, said Leandra—go on and ask him.

Will I be seeing the real Mr. Tanady again, mister whoever you are? Or will he be sending you from now on?

I—uh—I don't know, he said, taken off guard, as he pulled on his smoke.

My Uncle Franz and Aunt MacMillan were replaced by imposters too, said Christine. They came to visit me in the hospital but I guess they didn't have the stomach to come and visit me themselves in that hellhole so they sent other people in disguise. Why does this happen to me? Am I so awful that nobody really wants to be with me?

No, said Ronald. Don't think that, that's not it at all, you are wonderful.

Dreamily she turned her head and held Leandra's hand.

I can count on at least one person being real, she sighed.

Leandra smiled lying under the sheet beside her, as she turned back to the man in the mask.

The imposters even knew what it was that we called them, she told him—Uncle Franz and Aunt MacMillan—the first name for him, the last name for her. They talked about their trip—said that they'd just come back from a trip to Sweden, but I knew that wasn't true. They tried to tell me all about Sweden in the hospital day room there, but I knew they hadn't really been in Sweden. It was my real Uncle and Aunt who had been to Sweden. I knew about that because they had written me letters about their vacation when I was in the hospital, and so I knew I wasn't the only person reading my mail. You know what I mean? In those awful hospitals they always read your mail.

Uh huh, he said, blowing smoke as she went on.

Anyway—they were the only ones who had tried to keep in touch with me besides my Mom and I was so happy when they wrote me they were coming up to the hospital to visit but I was really disappointed when I saw that it wasn't them—that they had sent someone else in their place. The imposters went on talking and I pretended that it was really them but they couldn't fool me, it wasn't the same as being with my real Uncle and Aunt. And then I figured it out. Uncle Franz and Aunt MacMillan lived really, really far away—and they didn't want to, or couldn't travel so far; so they hired these local imposters to come and see me in disguise—to cheer me up, to encourage me to get better. Once I figured that out I felt a lot better, I felt that they really loved me—because to pay for the imposters and to buy the costumes and to go to all the trouble to tell the two of them what to say and how to act must have been both very time consuming and very, very expensive. You know what I mean? You know?

Ronald laid his head back, smoking, listening. The smoke snaked around the room as Christine went on.

So anyway, even though they couldn't come visit me themselves, I knew that they loved me and I didn't feel so bad. You should have seen my Uncle and Aunt. All tall, blonde and blue eyed, making you think without a doubt that they were from Sweden. Uncle Franz was in fact born in Sweden. You really would look at both of them and immediately think—Sweden. That's why they said they

went to Sweden—to visit Uncle Franz's brothers and his sisters—
and what's amazing is that this imposter Franz could really spin
stories about Sweden, as if he'd actually been there himself—he
went on about Sweden this, and Swedish that, and how wonderful
and beautiful it was and I was amazed at all the details he was able
to add. The real Franz must have taught him well. It was almost
like being with the real Uncle Franz and Aunt MacMillan—even
their makeup was perfect. Hey, Mr. Tanady, or whoever you are.
Where do you think we look like we're from? If someone looked
at us, where would they think we're from?

I don't have the slightest idea, said Ronald, his smoke layering
the room.

Aw come on, give it a guess?

I don't know, England?

I have a test for you—this will prove that you're not really Mr.
Tanady. Ready?

Sure, fine.

He brought the cigarette to his mouth and took a deep drag as
she spoke.

What are you most guilty about?

What?

Leandra squeezed Christine's hand under the sheet.

I said—What did Mr. Tanady do as a child that he's most guilty
about?

He looked at her, crushed out his cigarette, and immediately
propped himself up on his elbows.

Christine—you know the answer to that question as well as I do.
Do you mean to say, that if I was an imposter, you'd repeat what
I told you in confidence?

I didn't say I'd repeat it, I'm not going to tell you what I know, that would ruin the test—I just said tell me what it was.

He looked down and took the sheet between his fingers and looked her in the eye and said, I don't want to talk about that—I'm not in the mood. I should never have told you that to begin with.

You mean about what you did in school.

Right.

Then you don't know. See? You're not Mr. Tanady.

Christine, enough of this crazy talk—I am Ronald Tanady, I don't understand what's the matter with you.

Crazy? she said, sitting up. Are you saying that I'm crazy?

He swept a hand across his forehead.

No I didn't call you crazy—I just said this is enough of this kind of talk.

What kind of talk? Crazy talk?

Okay, fine—yes! Enough of this crazy talk!

If you think I talk crazy, then you must think I am crazy. Mr. Tanady would never say such a thing about me. Mr. Tanady is a true gentleman—see you just proved you're not him. I know Mr. Tanady. He'd never call me crazy. He respects me. Plus you didn't know what he's ashamed of. That's two strikes against you.

Ronald sat up and swung his legs off the bed, putting the ashtray and cigarettes on the vanity and then he got back under the sheet with Christine putting his hands on her and said, How about some more now Christine? Your—crazy talk has gotten me all worked up.

Okay, okay—sure. Come on.

She put her hands on him and he came to her. The interrogation about whether he was Mr. Tanady had given Ronald new energy.

There! he groaned, pushing hard—there! I'll teach you who is Mr. Tanady and who is not Mr. Tanady—tell me after we're done some other person could do this to you like me! I will punish you forever for doubting that I am me—there! There! There!

There!

And at last, when they were done and they just lay there together in the bed, barely touching each other as before, Leandra snuggled close to Christine and Christine was glad to have her secret lying right there next to her, a secret that the fake Mr. Tanady knew nothing about. Christine liked secrets. Her world was full of secrets—in fact, to her, the whole world, in a way, was just one big secret. She turned to Mr. Tanady. His profile cut across her door.

Hey, she said—hey Mr. Fake Tanady.

He pulled on his smoke before answering.

What?

I lied to you before.

You lied about what?

I lied to you about my relatives visiting me in the hospital—I have neither Uncle Franz nor an Aunt MacMillan.

What?—he said, turning to her.

I just made that story up—to get you going. There's no Uncle Franz and no Aunt MacMillan—What kind of a name is MacMillan for a Swede? You ought to have picked that up, and challenged me on it.

I didn't feel like it's my place to challenge you, he said. MacMillan—what do I care what nationality MacMillan is? I don't even know myself.

MacMillan is Irish. And if MacMillan is Irish, what kind of a name is Franz? You ought to have challenged me on that too.

I told you why I didn't.

Hah! I got you on that, but you still don't know what Tanady told me he was guilty about. You're not Tanady—you know what?

What?

How dare you come and do all this to me when you're pretending to be someone else. This here is intimate—what we just did is intimate stuff—how dare you?

She sat up, her eyes fiery.

It just hit me! The balls of you—pretending to be someone that I cared for! Get out of my house—pay me the money that you owe me, and then get the fuck out of here!

But I am Ronald. I am Mr. Tanady, he said, standing by the bed and clutching at his clothes balled up on the chair. You are—you really are—here, take your damn money!

He pulled her money from the pocket of his pants and threw it on her bed.

She snatched it up, counting it quickly and said again, You are not Mr. Tanady because you don't know what he told me he was most guilty about! Well—don't ever come to see me again—and tell Mr. Tanady—I don't want to see him again either—

Ronald pulled on his pants.

Okay, Ronald said—you want to know what I'm most guilty about? That I would never tell anyone else about and don't like to talk about?

Yes I want to know! I want you to be the real Mr. Tanady!

He shuffled around, struggling to pull his pants up as he spoke.

Bully! he said, I feel guilty about having been a bully in grammar school! I did terrible things as a bully, and I felt justified in my behavior by my victim's weakness. I saw being a bully as life lessons for the weaker kids. Now that I have my own kids, and I see how hard they are trying to be liked, I'm terribly ashamed of what I did.

When he had his pants up, he buckled them closed. Then he put on his shirt. Finally he sat down to get on his socks and shoes.

I—uh—I think Tanady could have told you that, said Christine softly, her sheets pulled up over her head. That doesn't prove you are the real Tanady.

But you just had to make me say it, didn't you, he said, pulling on his socks. Christine, I don't know what what's going to happen to you. And I don't care what you say about me never coming back. Against my better judgment, I like you and I plan on being here next week, same day, same time. Hopefully you will have come to your senses by then.

He smiled over at her, and she spoke as he tied his shoes.

Yes, yes, okay—but tell the real Mr. Tanady I want him. Not you.

Sure.

I'm sure you can find somebody else to fuck. Are you married? Ronald's married.

No, I'm not married.

What did you do in school growing up? Were you a bully like Ronnie?

No I was not a bully. I was just a kid.

I never went to school, Christine said, pulling an arm out from under the sheet and laying her hand out flat. She was still holding Leandra's hand in the other.

Oh no?

No—I was in the hospital for all those years—Mr. Tanady

knows. Talk to him, he'll tell you all about it—or do you want to stay and hear it all from me?

He gave her a long look from where he sat on the edge of the bed.

I don't know, Christine—the look of you is making me want to stay a little longer.

If you want to—I can do it again—but it'll cost you another fifty.

I—I don't have another fifty dollars—

Her arm slowly came up and she raised her head.

Hey you know, she said, there is something you can tell me about that I never talked to Mr. Tanady about.

What's that?

What was it like to go to school? All those years?—Sitting in all those classes at all those desks with all those teachers through the years?

When you're young it seemed like it would never end.

Really? My twenty years went fast.

I seems to me it would.

There were times when they tried to school me, they had a classroom there. When I was awake they tried to teach me things. But it was a lost cause.

Why, he said, leaning over on one hand.

My mind couldn't keep anything in. It was all fuzzy. I remember looking around the class room just taken away with all the colors and the look of the room and all the stuff in the room. When you spend half your life asleep everything looks fairly amazing when you're finally awake. It's like—it's like—it's like it's all too much, you know? What's it like when you grow up awake all the time?

You're not awake all the time. You sleep at night.

You know what I mean! she said, slapping her hands onto the sheet.

I don't really know how to describe it. It's like—you're awake is all. Like you're awake right now. Come on, you know how it feels. You're messing with me again—

No, I'm not—what about the years passing—what's it like to be awake and feel all the years passing?

It just happens. You go from one day to the next and go through the grades and you get bigger and the work gets to be more complicated and—you just pass through the years.

Are you afraid to tell me what it was like?

Afraid?

You don't want to tell me what I missed all those years.

I guess you missed a lot—

You don't like talking about this do you?

It's not how you usually talk.

She half-sat up.

Usually? How would you know how I usually talk? You're not Mr. Tanady, you've never been here before. You look afraid. Why are you afraid?

I'm not afraid. I just think that's a lot to have to explain to you—what school was like, and to have the years pass by, and all that.

She laid herself back onto the pillow and squeezed Leandra's hand.

Well, okay—if you don't have another fifty I guess now you will be going. But don't be scared of me there's nothing to be scared of—

I know, I know. I'm not scared, Christine.

You know what I would be scared of? said Christine.

No what?

To be on Mount Everest with all the dead bodies that are laying all around.

What dead bodies? Where? he said as he slipped on his jacket.

Mount Everest. There are over two hundred dead bodies on Mount Everest—people that fell climbing or passed out or just froze to death. They're still there—they're just sitting there, laying there—when you climb up you pass them. They never change. They just lay there. No years pass by them. They are like rocks and stones. Imagine a place like that? What an awful place that would be—lying there, your eyes burned out, just blank holes staring up at the skies, forever.

I have to go Christine.

Oh. All right. Tell Ronald that I said hello and that he better get his fat butt in here next week.

I will. Take care of yourself Christine.

You still look afraid. Are you?

I'm not afraid.

Want me to show you out?

No need. Goodbye Christine.

Goodbye Sir.

He went out the door and as the door clicked shut behind him, Christine rolled over and embraced Leandra and cried and cried until she finally fell asleep for the night, under the single sheet, with her light burning on the vanity, and Leandra whispering all night into her dream, Don't worry, I love you, even if none of them do. I do, you know I do, I do, I do.

6 – Mount Everest II

DON'T GET ME WRONG. CHRISTINE IS VERY GOOD AT WHAT SHE DOES; what she gets paid for. But what is this nonsense about me being somebody else—me being Mr. Tanady in disguise? You're not Mr. Tanady, she said—you're not Mr. Tanady! Who are you? Where did she get that from? Oh, I know she spent a lot of years in the big crazy house in Hebron. But I thought they let her out of there when she was better. I thought they kept people in when they have big problems. Christine seems to have big problems—but she is good at what she does. I don't even mind pushing my way into that shithole of a house to get up to her room. The place stinks to high heaven, but once you get there, her room is clean. And she does smell good. Let me tell you.

So, like I told her, I was a bully in school. I'm not proud of it. I don't know why Christine had to force me to tell her that when I was with her—I don't know why Christine says or does a lot of the things she does. But I am ashamed and guilty about having been a bully. I know I made the younger kids' lives at my school miserable when they ought to have been enjoying growing up. I know I made the little kids fear coming to school each day. I was that bad. But I was miserable at the time too. That's what started it. I know that Christine thinks everybody needs to know this about me, so—here's the whole story.

Growing up, I was a big kid for my age. I had hands twice the size of other kids. My whole body was twice the size of other kids. I've grown out of that and now I'm no bigger or smaller than the average man. But I had a big growth spurt as a kid. I was just way ahead of everybody else. I felt really funny about it. I knew they thought I was a freak. They never said anything but I imagined what they were thinking; here comes Ronald the giant, with his fat hands. I wouldn't have anything to do with them because I thought they were always looking down on me. I've always been good at knowing what people are thinking about me, even if they never say a thing. That went on for several grades, and I just took it. The boys wouldn't play with me at recess. I never got picked for a team. The girls didn't play with me either. I used to spend all recess just sitting alone on the blacktop over by where the girls played jump rope and I'd just watch them the whole time, and all the other things they did. And it was like I wasn't really there. I felt that somehow everything was one step removed from me. I felt like I didn't belong there or anywhere. So I stayed far away from everybody and after a while I just sat alone at the corner of the playground every day, pounding the blacktop with stones and breaking off pieces from the corner where the blacktop ended and the dirt began. I sat like that for every recess, far away and alone from everybody else. Even when I was close to the other kids, either in class, or in gym, it was like I was somehow far, far away, so I made it be like it was; I made myself be far away. And so I always sat far away. The sun would come down on me as I sweated at my work, breaking up the blacktop. To this day I wonder—is that corner still there? All chipped away, to this day? My bet is that if I went to that corner today and looked, it wouldn't be the same since they have probably resurfaced the playground by now. But still, I'm tempted to stop by there and look sometime, but I worry that the people who live across the street from there would see and say things to each other, hiding behind their drawn curtains.

What's that weirdo doing?

What's that weirdo there for?

We had better call a cop, just to be sure. Yes we had better.

Go to the phone and call—I'll keep an eye on this weirdo—

They would talk like that and I'd end up in trouble. So I don't stop to look around, to see if the blacktop is still chipped in the corner of that schoolyard, where the dirt starts.

It was the summers that I lived for. Then I got to hang around with the bigger kids in the neighborhood. None of them went to my school. None of them knew how I felt about it. I felt close to them. I felt like I belonged. Summers were great and everything pulled in closer around me and there was no distance between me and the other kids and I felt real then; not like in school, where I was the giant surrounded by all the tiny kids. Instead, I felt among equals; and they treated me like one of them. It didn't matter that I was years younger. They liked me for who I was—what I was—not something that I had to be ashamed of like it was in school. With my summer friends, I was not a giant. I was just a regular kid. Then, one year, a summer came that was just so good—so sunny, so carefree. And when the start of school started to come up—the start of sixth grade—and as the days counted down toward the end of summer, I felt low, trapped in a hole, knowing that soon this perfect summer would be over and I would be the giant again that no one wanted to have anything to do with. I would be in that playground again, sitting at the corner of the blacktop, pounding it with my stone, breaking it up, all alone.

Look at the big freak, they would all be thinking.

Look at the big weird freak sitting there.

So here I was facing it all again. The night before school started I lay in bed and I cried real tears. It had been a really great summer. And there I was crying real tears over it. So it came to me; like a bat to the head; an idea; a feeling that came over me. If the kids at my school thought that I was a freak, a giant, a giant I would be. A giant to be feared; and feared I would be. My tears set into a hard mask that came over my face; a hard, dark mask that I would wear from that night on with pride. When I went to sleep, I did so knowing my past was gone. And my future was about to roll over me. And it would be different. I would no longer let the little kids push me away to that lonely corner. And something in me knew this was what growing up was; where I had passed some gate into the future.

I chose to be feared, and I targeted those who I knew were thinking I was a freak; the little, cute ones who played their ball games and king-of-the-mountain games and tag and all those playground games. There were one or two damned little runts running around like they thought they were big shits, that I held for special treatment. I knew who I would target; one named Mark, his last name was not important—but Mark thought he ran the school and so the first thing I did to him was when he was running the bases in a game of baseball that I was left out of, I ran into the game from the side and tripped him. He sprawled face-first into the dirt and before he could get up I pulled him up by the hair and called him a name so bad that I can't bear to repeat it; his friends just stared at me without believing what I had just done. Mark struggled free and tried to stand up to me but I punched him hard in the stomach. He doubled over, the wind knocked out of him, and I pushed him down in the dirt. I walked through the very center of the game, laughing. I went to the plate, got a bat and started swinging it, and I yelled.

I'm in the game now—I'm on this team now and I'm up.

They looked at me as I stepped up to the plate and swung the bat, slicing through the afternoon air. They were all trying to put their brave faces on after what I'd done to their Mark.

What's the matter? Scared that I'm in the game? Throw already—or you'll get what that other kid just got. Maybe worse even.

Finally the pitcher threw some balls my way. He struck me out after the first three pitches.

Okay, he said toward me. You're out. Next up!

No! I yelled, shaking my fist. I'm staying up here until I hit one!

From behind came a voice; the damned catcher had dared speak up.

You're out, he said. There are rules, you know the rules—

I spun around and grabbed him by the hair, he was like a rag doll in my hands and I felt power—real power—I felt like I felt in the summer hanging out with the big kids—and I shook him like a rag doll and threw him down and turned and swung the bat and yelled to the pitcher.

Come on! Pitch!

He looked around. The whole team looked at him; and slowly, slowly, he pitched.

And he pitched; and went on pitching—and I knew that they were now all afraid of me. From that day on, I terrorized those two boys every day on the playground. I'd go up to them, follow them around wherever they went, and push them down or sucker punch them whenever I felt like it. The others didn't do a thing, they just felt lucky that I hadn't picked them. Now and then I'd go after one of the others to keep them on their toes, but the main ones I bullied were Mark and the catcher, Kevin. Bullying made me feel like a big man; and the year flew by, and what fun I had. Once I tripped Mark in the classroom when he was walking up to the board, I stuck my foot out in his way and he and his papers went flying and all the teacher did was send me to the principal's office. From then on I just went after them in the playground until they were scared to death to go out at recess. And I noticed that Mark—the one I hated the most—Mark stopped playing the games at recess and stayed to himself around the corner of the school building. It was like those two little runts took my place at the asphalt corner that I used to chip away at. Instead I had chipped away at those two little runts. I had chipped away at them all year, until they feared me—until everybody feared me—and it felt so good. It felt like it was summer, all year round. I figured that they were pretty miserable. And that was how it should be. Other people should be miserable, not me! Then I noticed that Mark started being out sick a lot. I noticed that sometimes he didn't even come out for recess, staying in the classroom instead. When he wasn't around, I went after Kevin—and a few others instead. But they were nothing like Mark. Mark was my best victim by far. He started doing really bad on tests and he started to forget his homework and when he was called to the board he couldn't do his work. Good! Good, I thought. And the next couple of years went like that until eighth grade was over, and we all moved on to different schools. After that I never saw Mark or Kevin again, but every day I thanked God for sending them to me, to save me from how miserable and alone I was. I suppose I loved them in some twisted way. I loved their weakness, and the way that they crumpled under my tormenting. They were like my best friends. Later in life, I had mostly forgotten about it but then I started remembering the look on Mark's face, like a hunted animal—like a cornered, trapped animal—and with that image in my mind, I thought about what I probably had created. He may have ended up sitting at the corner of the blacktop at the next school he went to. He may have thought that the others were all talking about him—looking at him—refusing to have anything to do with him, terrified about which one of them would come and bully him. I'm guessing that he feared the others. He probably imagined that it would all happen again sooner or later. But he was probably still too small—too puny—to do anything about it. So he may have looked for things that were smaller and weaker and then him, to terrorize. Maybe he spent time alone and one night it came to him—he made the conscious decision, as I had done, to become a bully himself. But he couldn't go after the kids in school—he couldn't bully in high school the way I had bullied in grammar school, he wasn't big and strong enough. He realized that he needed something weaker, something smaller—cats, dogs, frogs, salamanders—little kids living down the block in the neighborhood in the summer. With those little kids, he might have been the big kid on the block. Just like me, he would have pulled their hair, he pushed them down into the dirt and made them sit in a hole, threatening to bury them. He'd take a kitten to the cellar and beat it and whip it to where it would end up sitting in the coal bin, its eyes shining, fearful in the black coal dust. He'd throw rocks at the dogs in the pen out back and he'd get his father's shotgun in the summer and take it out and shoot down saplings, stray cats, squirrels and crows. When the migrating birds flew far above the treeline, he'd shoot up into the stream, and birds would veer off, tumble and fall dead to the ground. And he went on to do worse things, much worse things. I imagine that he ended up hurting some people really bad and that leads me to wonder where is he now; where Kevin is now, where are all the others now?

We are living parallel lives, unseen and unknown to each other but we all come from the same point in time, the same beginnings. But I know this to be true, wherever he is, Mark is a monster today. Because of me, he hates himself and torments others, and those around him hate him just as much. If he hasn't been caught, he is still doing awful, twisted things. And it is all because of me. Yes; it is all because of me. I know it is going on right now somewhere. He's somewhere doing terrible things to someone, and I regret having created this monster. That's what I imagine—that Ronald Tanady created a monster. It has become all that I think about at night in the quiet—when it's just like it was that night I lay crying in bed and it came over me to be a monster. I now know that monsters make monsters. Thank God there are things in my life that help me forget about what Mark is doing now—things that help me think that I am just an innocent man, like everyone else around me. All I ever wanted was to be like everybody else. All I ever wanted was to be able to spend time with nice people, like Christine. This is why I thank God for Christine. She delivers me from myself. She accepts me as myself. But sometimes I don't know about her. Like tonight when she thought I was somebody else. It might be good to be somebody else. Somebody who hadn't done what I'd done. Someone who wasn't or isn't a monster, because once a monster, always a monster. If Mark is really out there, then the past is still there. It lives just as he lives. Nothing changes. I want to be innocent, but I never will be. Those kids will never forget me. And as long as they remember me that way, that's the way I am, no matter what I do to change, no matter the number of times that Christine takes me into her embrace. And so they are, always there on that playground, their eyes full with terror. It will never be over. It never was over. I was a monster, and so I will be one forever. And there will continue to be more and more and more.

7 – Deshler Borough Hall

THELMA SAT IN THE KITCHEN, THE PLASTIC BLACK AND WHITE TV flickering and balanced on a stack of garbage up above the sink. Christine came down from her room, uncovered another chair and eased into it.

Did you fill out that appeals form Mom? asked Christine.

What appeals form? said Thelma, staring dreamily up at the TV.

The one I got at borough hall the other day—remember? I went down there to ask about changing our deadline to get the place cleaned up?

Oh, that form. No, I haven't filled it out yet.

Christine produced a pen from her pocket. She waved it to get her mother's attention.

Where is the form, she said—I'll fill it out. I want to get it back to them today.

I don't know where it is. In here somewhere, I suppose.

Christine slapped her knees hard.

Stop looking at that TV and look at me! she said. We need to find that form now! Where's your head?

Thelma turned to Christine and pointed at her.

How dare you talk to me like that, she snarled, poking her finger, her eyes tiny pinpoints scribed onto her face.

Never mind how I talk to you—find that form now!

Heavily Thelma rose from her chair and, turning, she moved her thin arms over the trash atop the table, searching. As she searched, she spoke.

If your Father were alive you wouldn't be talking to me like that Christine. He'd never stand for it.

Christine reached up and switched off the TV, saying Sure—sure. Listen, there are a lot of things here he wouldn't be standing for if he were alive.

Thelma continued searching for the piece of paper, a scowl come over her face, her arms moving like the pincers of some praying mantis over the garbage as she turned to Christine and said What is that supposed to mean?

It means that this house wouldn't be in this shape if he had lived. This problem wouldn't be happening and a lot of other things would have gone different too! I cannot believe you lost that form!

I didn't lose it! I just can't find it right now. But listen—

She turned to her daughter and crossed her arms.

What other things? What are you trying to say to me Christine? Why don't you come right out and say it?

I don't have to say anything right out, Mom. I don't! You know as well as I do how different things would have been if he hadn't crashed that truck of his! Things fell apart—everything fell apart—but listen, find that form, Mom—if you don't find it I'll have to go down and get another one—damn it anyway!

Christine turned from her mother and kicked her way through the trash, making her way back towards her room.

Where are you going? Thelma yelled after her.

To my room! I need to relax! Let me know when you find the form.

I—

Shut up and just find it!

Christine squeezed past the stacks of trash and went up the stairs and into her room, slamming the door behind her.

Oh Leandra, she said, leaning her back against the door. Leandra if only you were here with me now, she whispered, head bowed.

It was one of the bad days. Leandra had not come to her this day. It was just Christine, the four walls to her room, an empty bed and the deadline for the form. What would she do when the deadline came? Where would she and her mother go? And was it true about her Father? Yes, of course, it was all true—everything would have been different, it would have been better. Christine went to the vanity and sank into her chair. There was no one in the mirror but her. She spoke to her face reflecting back to her, her lips moving as she listened to the words coming back to her from the mirror; words that wound around her and fixed her there in a vision that came from behind her. She could see her father Martin in her reflection. Their lips moved together. He spoke to her through their lips.

There's no point in going after your mother, honey. What is done is done. There's no going back. There is just going forward. Now go down and take care of that borough hall; that damned stinking Deshler borough hall. I'll show you how it ought to have been done; how I would do it.

A man came out of the mirror and took Christine by the hand and together they headed back downstairs. Christine followed without protest. She wanted to see what her father would do.

They went down the stairs so fast that some of the trash on the stairs collapsed and followed them down in a heap. Her father went to Thelma, who was still hunched over the table, searching for the appeals form. Martin stood beside Thelma, turned and spoke to Christine.

Get your mother ready, we're taking her to borough hall.

Mom, breathed Christine, gripping her mother's kitchen chair—get your socks and shoes on, we're going to borough hall.

Thelma stared at the man with Christine and turned white. Go somewhere? said her mother—I can't go somewhere. I never go anywhere, you know that.

Thelma had not been out of the house in months. She had neither socks, nor shoes on for months. Christine sat her in her kitchen chair. She raised up a foot. The socks and shoes were there under the kitchen table. She put them on her mother like she'd imagine putting them on a child of hers and spoke soothingly to her mother with Martin standing there nodding approvingly.

We're going down to borough hall to fix our problems, he said. We're going down to fix our problems the way they ought to be fixed.

Our problems?

Yes, said Martin—I am here to show you both what it means to solve a problem.

But you are—

Dead? Who me? No, I was never dead. I was, so therefore I still am. Now I am here to show you.

Thelma stood up next to Christine and held her hand. Together they shuffled to the front door and went out. Martin snatched up the car keys as he passed the bowl by the front door.

We are going to lock the house, right? said Thelma.

No, said Martin—it'd be a blessing if someone were to come in while we were gone and take out all the shit that you've got in there. You've got too much shit in there. Why did you let all that shit pile up? And look at my yard! My God!

The yard was piled high with boxes, bags, and loose trash, and the walkway to the road where the car was, was just a thin path cut through the rotting mass.

No wonder the neighbors are complaining, said her father. Just look at this mess; and the smell! It stinks to high shit heaven! Come on, get in the car here.

Christine's father pulled Thelma by the hand around to the driver's side and opened the back door and the old woman got in without protest. Martin closed the door over and pointed to the great gash running the length of the side of the car and said How did you ruin this car? Where did it get that gash? Christine, tell me.

She didn't know the story but it started to come out and as she listened to it she began to know how the story went.

A truck hit me, she said—I was sitting at a red light and a truck came from the cross street and made a too-wide turn and his bumper ran along the side of the car, gashing it in as you see it.

Hmm, said her father—ever more you are the pitiful little innocent Christine, huh? Not your fault, as usual. Nothing is ever your fault.

His eye cut hers. She turned away and went around to the passenger side of the Lincoln and got in. Martin got into the driver seat and roared the car awake with a twist of the key. Thelma said from the rear view mirror, I haven't found the form yet Christine—I know you wanted me to find the form but I couldn't find it—

We won't need any damned form, said Martin, as he pulled the car out into the street with a roar. We just need—he fisted the steering wheel as he went on—we just need these. He lifted a clenched fist towards the roof of the car.

Houses lots, poles, fences and hedges flowed by as if projected onto a screen. The car jolted and rocked over the railroad tracks down the street and Thelma remembered how Martin used to go down to those tracks and spend whole afternoons walking them away from her; but now he was back. He was back. She didn't want to think how because that might make him go.

The town came up around them as they moved; schools, traffic lights, other cars and large storefronts filled with dummies. There were no people in the streets; just fashionably dressed dummies looking out over the sidewalks from within their glass vanity rooms. They looked out at Christine as Martin spun the wheel and turned them into the borough hall parking lot; the building grey and turreted looking like a fortress. He parked them where it said five minute parking, in front of the main entrance door and Christine asked Will we be done in five minutes, and as he opened his door, Martin said, It would have been done in negative thirty years if I'd been here—see, the problem is I haven't been here yet.

But I'm here now. And it counts.

You will see.

It counts.

He got out and opened the back door and took Christine's mother by the hand and she stepped out in her bathrobe and Christine thought that she hadn't realized that Thelma was still in her bathrobe—and she said to her, Can you go in here in that bathrobe? and Martin said, sure she can—come on Thelma you can come around the car now, just like that.

Together they walked across the empty parking spots and up the slate steps of the old building between overgrown and unattended hedges and the unwatered dying flowers, and Thelma stepped up and inside first with Martin holding the door open and Christine followed Thelma in as her father closed the door after them, coming in behind, and they saw the sign that said Code Enforcement. It was dark and shadowy in the old building, and Martin took his wife by the arm and eased her over to the clerk's window. A low cut man in brown shoes, a loose suit and a brushed back head of hair stiffly stood up, came to the window, put his face to the hole in the glass, and spoke through it.

Can I help you folks?

Yes, said Christine's father, as he pulled his wife closer to him by the arm. Just look at this pitiful old woman—would you put this pitiful old woman out of her house and onto the street?

The man pushed back his hair and thrust out his nose through the hole in the glass so sharply that it caused Christine to flinch back suddenly.

Who's trying to do that? he asked—Who's trying to put that old lady out on the street? Fill me in about what you're talking about. I can't help you if I don't know what you're talking about—

Christine's father swept his hand across and gripped his wife's arm tighter.

Next week they're coming to inspect her house, he said—and then they're going to put her out—

Oh, said the man, throwing his head back. This is the hoarder case on Wilson. You're the Zidars. Oh, I know. Yes—there have been multiple complaints received and multiple warnings given—

What's your name son, barked Martin, shutting the poor man down.

My—my name? Why do you want my name?

Because I'll need it when I speak to your boss.

What are you going to speak to my boss about? grimaced the shoeshined man.

Because you're calling this poor woman names—hoarder, you say—well she's no hoarder—just needs a little slack cut to give her time to tidy the place up. You—

Sir, said the man, raising a hand—there's been an order issued and a notice given. They're going out to inspect—I don't know why you're giving me such a hard time, but she's had multiple warnings—I suggest you take your energy back home and use it to clean up the place. The whole street is up in arms! And, may I remind you, they're all taxpayers—

No, you wait a minute, let me finish son—

I'm not your son, said the man, lifting a finger, and no, you let me finish—the taxpayers on the block are concerned and our job here is to address whatever it is that the taxpayers get concerned about.

This woman here is a taxpayer too. Listen, we're wasting enough time here already. Get me your boss. You're just a flunkie.

Her father rolled his eyes and looked away, her mother's eyes on the floor. The man in the window snapped, Fine! and turned away and shuffled his shoeshine back towards a door at the side of the room behind the glass, knocked, and went in.

Now, said Martin to Christine and Thelma—now we're getting somewhere. Bosses get to be where they are by having a brain—not like this flunkie. Listen—Christine, I need you to pipe up too. Pipe up and speak up for your mother.

I think you're doing just fine, said Christine, looking into his eyes.

As they waited for the boss, Christine looked around, and suddenly found herself in her room, back at the house. As if was the most natural thing to do, she went down to see if Thelma had found the appeals form that they'd end up needing. She went down the stairs, stumbling over the trash that had fallen earlier on her way up, went into the kitchen, and found Thelma sitting on her chair, clutching a piece of yellow paper in her hand, gazing up as always at the little black and white TV. Christine entered and excitedly pointed to the paper.

You've found it Mom? Is that the form? There in your hand?

Thelma's head turned as her body remained motionless aimed towards the TV flickering atop the trash, and she spoke in a near whisper.

No, she said—this is not it. I can't find it. This is the notice that they gave me saying they were going to inspect. I can't find the appeals form. I'm sorry.

Christine stepped up and reached and switched the TV off, then laid a hand on her mother's shoulder and spoke as Thelma looked up.

Okay Mom, get your shoes and socks on, we're going down to borough hall to get a new form, both of us.

Why should I come with you? You went by yourself before.

Because I think it's the right thing to do. Come on, get up. Here are your shoes and socks—put them on.

Meanwhile up at borough hall, Christine Martin and Thelma were still waiting and watching through the glass wall with the speaking hole in it for the door to the boss's office to open. As he rubbed his nose, Martin wondered aloud What's taking them so long? What is the damned problem? They're so worried about those other damned taxpayers, but what about us? What about us—why aren't they worried about us?

He rapped on the glass hard and shouted through the hole.

Hurry up! We don't have all day!

Meanwhile back at the house, Christine put the socks and shoes on her mother thinking she had just done this once before; now why was she doing it again? She felt so dizzy as she tied the shoes that she barely could get them tied. What was the problem? she wondered, what—

Finally at borough hall, a watery-eyed woman came out from the office, the shoeshine boy following her, and she came up to the window gripping the counter hard.

I hear you've got a complaint about Mister Barber here, she barked—what is it?—he says that you're the ones being rude and annoying, so before you even say anything about him, don't you dare be rude or annoying to me or I will have security show you the door. Is that understood?

Her eyes burned watery red into Martin's, demanding an answer.

Rude? he snapped—Rude and annoying? Us? No, but I could say the same thing about Mister Barber-pole here—is that what your little flunkie said? We're rude?

His name is Mister Barber, she snapped. And he's not a flunkie he's a—

Never mind him, said Martin, pointing sharply. He's not important. Here's what's important—we are trying to give this poor old woman here a little more time to tidy up her place before you inspect it—how about a couple of months? Give her a month—or two.

Sir, I don't think you ought to use that tone—

Christine and Thelma pushed past the chair and TV and trash bags, and headed for the door. Christine snatched up the keys to the Lincoln from the bowl to the side and they went out and as they started down the front steps Thelma held back.

Aren't you going to lock the house?

No, said Christine—it'd be a blessing if someone were to come in while we were gone and take out all the stuff that you've got in there. You've got too much stuff in there.

Having heard this someplace before, Thelma nodded and went down the narrow walk through the front yard garbage toward the car.

And no, there won't be any extensions, said the watery-eyed woman back at Martin—I checked the computer before I came out here. Your poor old lady has had nine warnings issued over a two-year period. The tenth warning is the final warning. There can be no appeal on a final warning. The city inspectors are scheduled to arrive next week to inspect the place and it better be cleaned out by then so you should be using your energy at home to clean up the mess, instead of coming down here and repeatedly harassing my staff.

Christine's father fumed as if smoke was coming out his ears. The shoeshine boy stood smiling behind the watery-eyed woman, her mouth set in a line and her eyes on Father's.

Christine and Thelma got into the car and pulled away after Christine once more surveyed the great gash that the truck had given her and she knew that someone had said something about the damage just earlier today but she had not been in the car earlier and it was just her and her mother there, so who—

Okay. We're done with you now! said Martin into the hole in the glass partition. Enough from you! I want to see your boss!

My boss is the Mayor—he's upstairs, said the woman, folding her arms. But you need an appointment. Go up and see his secretary and see if she will give you an appointment—he won't see you today—but at least I'll have you out of my hair!

Oh, he'll see us today—and you and your boy here will be in for a load of trouble.

I don't think so, she sniped, tossing her head.

We'll see, her father replied.

The three of them turned and headed through the shadows toward a big sign that said Deshler Mayor's Office.

Big deal, muttered Martin—big deal Mayor—well he's just a man, like me—

The town flowed up and around Christine and Thelma as they drove into it and Christine gripped the wheel and said, Mom, we're going to make a big stink today! We're going to make a big stink and that's why I wanted you to come along. I want them to see the sweet little person that they want to throw out into the street.

Sweet little person? oozed Thelma. What a nice thing to say—

Well, that is true Mom—but here comes borough hall—damn there's no close parking places. God, we got to find one—

Under the sign that said Deshler Mayor's Office there was a

bespectacled young woman in big hair sitting at a desk. She looked up, but Martin spoke roughly first.

We need to see the Mayor now, he said, lowering his gaze onto the woman. The people at the code enforcement window downstairs said we needed to see the Mayor today.

The young woman looked up at him, her liquid blue eyes swimming inside her golden rims.

The Mayor is not seeing anyone today, she said. I can make you an appointment for next week—

No! barked Martin, making the young woman jump—we need to see him today. There's no time, we—

Can I help you? said a smooth voice behind them. Father turned to the voice. A tall man stood there.

Who are you? said Father—another flunky I suppose?

I—I am no flunky, said the tall suited man standing there, his face reddening. I am the deputy Mayor and you seem to be in need of some help.

Yes—I need help—actually this old woman with me needs help. The town is going to put her out in the street and we're here to put a stop to it.

Oh really? So tell me, what's the story? said the tall man, touching a finger to his chin.

Father told him the whole story.

Christine and Thelma finally found a parking space a full city block away from the borough hall. Mother, did you see that there's a car just like ours parked in front of the borough hall's door? Said Christine—I thought ours was the only one. Without waiting for an answer, she dashed over and dropped money in the meter.

Funny, said the deputy Mayor when Father was done—it's simple to handle this, he said.

The coins dropped into the meter.

It looked like it had the same kind of dent across the side as ours too—

All you have to do is fill out an appeals form, said the deputy Mayor—we have them right here in this file—

No! shouted Father, turning back to the young woman sitting at the desk. You, he said to her—you buzz the Mayor and tell him we need to see him right now—right now!

Christine and Thelma walked toward borough hall. Thelma wore a smile and looked all around—she had not been out of the house for so long.

I can't, said the young woman. I'm sorry you'll have to make an appointment.

As Father opened his mouth to bark at her, the deputy Mayor touched his arm.

Sir, just calm down. Do as she says—use the appeals form—

Christine and Thelma turned the corner toward the borough hall door. A large earsplitting garbage truck went by, as Christine spoke up loud.

Almost there, Mom—almost there.

Father yelled No! Now! and rushed around the desk, and kicked in the Mayor's door. Sitting before him was a large white-shirted man with thick black hair behind a large desk with only a newspaper spread out before him.

What is this? said the Mayor—who are you? Who said you could bust in here like this?

You! shouted Christine's father, advancing on the Mayor.

Keep your distance now—keep back, I warn you, said the Mayor, reaching down into a drawer.

You need to help us, said Father, advancing further, pointing; and Christine and Thelma's Jaws dropped as the startled ex-Marine Mayor stood and in one smooth sweeping motion the Mayor shouted Stop, pulled a forty-five from the desk, raised it and cocked it and fired a bullet into Martin's heart, killing him instantly.

As they came up the steps of borough hall, Christine heard the shot through the heavy stone walls—Did you hear that? she asked Thelma—did you hear that big bang from somewhere inside?

I heard nothing, dear, said Thelma.

What? I sure did Mom. Are you sure?

Sure. I heard nothing at all.

As they spoke they went up the three steps and through the tall black doors and headed for the window with the sign that said Code Enforcement; but suddenly, so suddenly, two policemen pushed their way past Christine and Thelma and went on further, running toward the sign that read Deshler Mayor's Office. The policemen had drawn their weapons and were shouting words and numbers into their radios that were meaningless to the women, and sirens blared outside, loud, shrill, shrieking too loud much too loud; and Christine's head rose from the vanity and she rose slowly and turned to her door, glad for some reason it was so quiet up here. She meant to go downstairs to see if her Mother had found the appeals form amidst all the trash in her rotting stinking kitchen yet; the rotting stinking kitchen that would not be, if only, if only, Father had lived on.

8 – Fregoli Delusion

FRANCIS SERDON WAS A BULKY MAN WITH HIS FACE PASTED ON LIKE IT was a mask. He wore a smile which was always intensified by the services of Christine, and without his knowledge, of her friend Leandra, who lay as a shade beside the two, and laid her hand on his heaving back at his peaks from the services of Christine. Like Lewis, and Tanady, he was a regular. Christine was troubled by what had recently happened to her. So troubled that when he was done, lying spent beside her, she had to say it; Francis—where were you Monday?

He turned to her, I was at work, he said, biting his lip; a bad habit.

Francis worked as a manager at a large drug manufacturer. What exactly he managed Christine didn't know. She didn't know if he actually had anything to do with the manufacturing of the drugs. But it didn't matter; he was a manager, with a shrew of a wife, and he could afford a regular once-a-week with Christine.

At work? she asked—at work all day?

Yep, he said, staring at the ceiling, his naked body fat, exposed, and disgusting to Christine; but this was how she made her money. She too stared upward as she spoke.

I saw you at the Seven-Eleven Monday morning. You weren't at work. You were watching me buy the papers, weren't you?

What?

You were at the Seven-Eleven pretending to be one of those Spanish guys who works behind the counter and you were spying on me buying my papers.

He raised himself up on one elbow and looked at her open-mouthed, the large gap in his teeth all black inside.

What? he said—what are you talking about?—Oh, I get it.

He let his head fall back on the pillow and put his hands together behind his head. She's off again, he thought, biting his lip. She is off again. He closed his eyes and listened.

Yeah, she said, you put on a disguise to look like one of the Spanish guys and you went there to watch me. But I'm confused, what'd you do with the real Spanish guy? Did you pay him to stay in the back while I was there? I know that they had to be in on it with you, Serdon. And where did you get such a good disguise?

He continued to chew on his lip, opening his eyes to the ceiling as she went on.

How did you get it to look so real? You even looked smaller—that guy is small—how do you make yourself look smaller like that? Can you tell me?

It isn't hard, he muttered with a smile. I got the costume from Party City.

Party City?

She glanced over at Leandra who smiled and nodded at her to go on and then she turned back to Serdon and asked, Party City? You can't get such a great disguise at Party City. They sell plastic bag costumes. This was a disguise. They're two different things—this is not Halloween. They only sell costumes around Halloween. You know something, Serdon?

What?

If you're going to watch me, why not just be yourself? I wouldn't mind running into you outside of this room, I'd say hi and we could even have a nice conversation. I wouldn't pretend to not know you. But in disguise—I wouldn't dare talk to you any more after you said what you said to me in that disguise. Why couldn't you just talk to me regular even if you felt you had to hide seeing me and be in disguise?

What did the guy selling you the papers say?

No! See there—it wasn't some guy—it was you!

What did I say?

You know. You were there.

He rolled over and reached out and gently fondled Christine's breasts.

Okay—but enough about that, he said—how about some more honey? I'm ready to go again—here feel down here, want to feel it—

No! She said, pushing his hand down. I want to know why you did what you did. Don't try and distract me—

But this is why I pay you honey—

She pushed his hand completely off her.

There'll be time enough for that later, she said—first I need to know why you are doing what you are doing. It wasn't just at the Seven-Eleven, it was also at my doctor's. I went for an examination on Tuesday and instead of him being there, you were there disguised as my doctor. I told you when I saw you there, I said, oh come off it Francis, be real—come out of that disguise. And you pretended to be confused and just told me to lie down and you examined me, my private parts, like a stranger—like a doctor. Why did you need to pretend to be a doctor to examine me, when you get to spend all the time you want down in my pussy every time we meet here in my room?

He lay open-mouthed, the back of his hand slapped on his forehead.

Christine, he said—Christine, I don't like it when you are like this. Snap out of it—

She raised herself on her elbow and pointed at him.

Snap out of what? Out of knowing the truth? Out of seeing the games you play on me? Listen I just want to know why you're doing these things. I want to know why you're following me around and watching me where I go when I leave my house—

He raised himself on the edge of the bed and sat naked with his back to her.

I don't know what you are talking about. If you are playing with me, please stop. This is a real turn off, Christine, he said. Stop the fooling around—

Fooling around? You think I'm the one fooling around? You're the one that's doing the fooling around here. Come on, tell me—how are you so good at what you do? How do you get the disguises? How do you get the real people to let you take their place?

What do you mean? To get the real people to do what?

Like the doctor or the news paper guy. On Tuesday when I went for the papers he was himself, he wasn't you. Not like on Monday where it was you pretending to be him. Where was he Monday when you were there? This is the amazing part—they must be in on it with you. This has to be a big conspiracy—why are you doing this to me? Why don't you leave me alone? Am I not enough for you when we are together here in my room? Why do you need me all the time?

He put his face in his hands. He hoped that this would pass. He wanted to do her again before he left. She was worth waiting for; she was good. In the meantime he just sat, chewed his lip, wiped at his face, and listened to her rattle on, hoping that she would come to herself soon.

The most amazing thing is what you did at the grocery store on Wednesday—do you remember what you did at the grocery store on Wednesday?

Sure, Christine, he groaned. I remember—if that's what you want to hear.

How did you do it? she said, her eyes bugging. It was amazing—I almost ran from the place throwing up, you so nearly blew my mind—

How did I blow your mind? he asked, perking up

When I was going up and down the aisles, she said staring into his eyes—the people in every aisle were all you in disguise—this is amazing, I remember thinking to myself. How did you do that? What kind of magic did you have? And you looked perfect—every one of you looked perfect—you were a frumpy old housewife, a young Asian girl, an old man wobbling on his walking, a nun—

A nun?

That's right—a nun! How many of those do you still see around nowadays?—but you already knew that.

Christine kneaded her soft belly to sooth herself as she got more and more agitated.

But I want to know how you did the most amazing thing you did—and, I swear to God Serdon, I won't have sex with you again, tonight or otherwise, unless you tell me how you did it. It was amazing—

Oh yeah, he said, turning his head to her. What was so amazing?

There wasn't just one nun, there was a group of nuns shopping together—three of them in all—

What? You—

No don't talk, listen—they were all really you, all of them at once—and you smiled at me. It was your smile but it was on all three of them at once—it was that smile you do when you come here—how did you do three people at once? All together next to one another? That is when I felt like throwing up—when I ran from the store. It was terrible, terrible—why are you doing all these things to me? Francis, tell me—how did you do it and why are you doing it?

He looked over at her vanity and saw that she had a bottle of pills sitting there. Christine always had pills lying around. He rose from the bed and reached for them and he glanced at the label, then said Hey listen Christine. Can I have a couple of these?

Oh? Them? Sure.

Thanks.

He took two of the pills and swallowed them down dry, then turned to her lying there naked on the bed.

Christine, you are really special, he said, and this is all a really great story, but can you snap out of it now? I want to have sex with you one more time before I leave, as you know my time here with you is quickly running out.

He put his hand atop her and she moved it away.

Not yet, we can't have sex yet. I'll give you the extra time if you want it. I just need to tell you more.

He threw his hands up and rolled his eyes, There's more? Jesus! What else did I do? I had no idea that I am so amazing!

She nodded emphatically.

Oh yes, there's more. Lots more. The other day I caught you pretending to be my mother. I had come in from the store and there you were, standing in the kitchen, looking exactly like Thelma. And I said to you, do you remember? I said, Francis? How did you get in here? What have you done with my mother? And you continued like you were worried about me and acted just like my mother does when she is all worried and you came and put your hand on my shoulder and said, Calm down dear, just like she says sometimes. But I just shoved her hand and said, But where is my real mother? Where? And you said, I am your real mother—and you told me again to just calm down. But what was I supposed to do? You had my real mother someplace else, under the house, or hidden back at your place, maybe in your garage—

Jesus Christ, Christine, said Serdon—where do you get all this?

Shut up, never mind, just listen! I'm not done—it was then I realized that if you could take over my own mother that you could take over me too—and if you took over me, then at least I'd know where the real people go when you take them over—so I said real loud Take me, Serdon! Take me, be me! And you sat down after looking real wild-eyed and you just pretended to cry just like my mother cries when she's feeling helpless and lost and I shouted down at you while you were hunched over the kitchen table and I said What's the matter? You don't have the guts to be me? Come on, come on—be me—but you just kept on crying and you said to me, Christine, my poor Christine, snap out of it—and you looked up at me with her face and it was too much, too much for me—so I pushed past her and ran up here and got right into bed.

She stopped there, and closed her eyes, but continued to violently knead her belly and her breasts. Serdon reached and took her by the wrist and stopped her.

Christine, open your eyes—stop playing with yourself like that—you're really turning me on. If you're not going to let me fuck you right now, just stop it!

She opened her eyes and looked at his crotch.

I can see that, she smiled. I can see your funny little underwear tent pole poking up.

Can we have sex now? he pleaded—that's what I came for, and I need to leave soon.

No not yet Francis, I want to know what you did with my Mother and the Nuns and the newspaper guy and all those people, and I want to know it now. And the disguises—how did you do the three nuns at once? Listen, Francis, this is making me sick—why can't you tell me? Why can't you just be a normal person and come up to me in the store and be yourself and say hello—and how dare you do this to my Mother—that was the worse. Where did you learn to cry real tears when you were pretending to be my Mother? Tell me, Francis, tell me. Tell me and I will feel better. Then, maybe then, we can think about a fuck.

Her hands moved towards his. His hand moved towards hers also.

I am magic, he said, writhing in discomfort. That is how I manage to do it all. I am magic. Okay Christine? Does that make you feel better?

Their hands moved together.

You are telling me nothing—but I feel better—come to me, Francis. Come to me. It is time.

He went onto the bed and got atop her and she spread her legs and finally they began to have sex. To him all the crazy talk was forgotten and forgiven as he focused on the thrusting of his hips; while Christine watched the white ceiling drift past like snow and went far away, farther away, until she was finally gone, high up in the mountains.

How did he do it, she thought as he held her tight and thrust hard into her—how did he do it? I will get it out of him one day—he will tell me—I will make him tell me—I know how to make him tell me—I do—I didn't tell him but he was the gas station attendant and the man behind the glass at the code enforcement bureau—I don't know how he is doing this, but he is—Green Boots—Green Boots—lying there dead for decades high atop Everest—funny, how it all comes back to Everest—there are bodies on Everest—there are bodies on Everest even as I lay here—Everest is there and there are bodies on it—how do they climb the damned thing—how do they just go by all those damned bodies like some battlefield from the middle ages like one of those movies where there's a war and a big battle and after the battle is over there are bodies laying around as far as the eye can see—

He pushed harder into her, so hard, so fast, her thoughts flowing faster.

—and the hero walks among the bodies and does what heroes do but the difference is there is moaning in the movie there are half dead people—but on Everest they're all dead laying around as far as the eye can see and Serdon is all those dead bodies and the climbers reach the peak—the peak—the peak—the peak above the dead—high above the dead—they conquer the dead—but three nuns—three nuns—three nuns—how'd he do three nuns—

Three nuns! she yelled, as Serdon finished.

Why the hell did you yell three nuns? he groaned, why the hell—?

But the question drained from him as he held on, his face buried in her hair over her shoulder. Slowly he released his grip on her and five minutes later he was dressing to leave and she was lying under the sheet, spent from all the talking before. Her troubles drained from her; they drained out of her and down into her mattress and down into her springs and down into the dark place beneath the floor. As he dressed she watched him, and when she was ready, she spoke to him in a relaxed manner, her voice smooth as silk; so smooth, so different, it shocked him.

You're good, Serdon, she said, smiling—you're good at everything you do—so you are a master of disguises too. So what if you never tell me how or why you do it? Just don't do it anymore, okay? When I'm in the store be yourself and come up and give me a friendly hug and kiss, all right—don't watch me all sneaky like you do. It isn't necessary you know—it isn't really necessary. Do that stuff to other people. With me you are fine to be yourself. You can come up and talk to me. I might even like it if you were to say hi to me and recognize me when we are away from this room. Okay?

He nodded as he buttoned his shirt and pulled on his jacket. He continued smiling at her. He took out his wallet and got out a fifty dollar bill and tossed it on the bed.

A bonus for tonight, he said. Next Thursday same time?

Yeah. Next Thursday, same time.

Okay bye. And thanks. And I'll just be myself from now on, I promise. No more disguises. If I see you, I'll be sure to come up and say Hi. Okay Christine?

Okay. Bye. And thank you.

No problem. Just don't worry about it anymore. Now go to sleep.

All dressed, he leaned over and pecked her on the cheek and she smiled. He turned and went through the door and went downstairs picking his way through the trash, rolling his eyes. He was glad to have had his release, but he was also glad to leave. She sure was good, and she was certainly worth it; she really was quite a woman—but three nuns? My God, three nuns; he laughed aloud as he got into his car and drove away.

9 – Mount Everest III

CHRISTINE IS A CHARACTER. SHE MAKES ME HORNY, THAT'S FOR SURE. But I've always gotten horny easy. Ever since I can remember. This is why my wife Marnie won't do for me. There's nothing sexy about her. Christine is the opposite. Christine reminds me of the women in the magazines I used to read when I was a kid; or at least at the pictures I used to look at. I forget the names of the magazines but they were smaller, really glossy, and full of the very best pictures of naked women. Christine could have been in one of those magazines—just laying there on the bed like she does. Just laying there—Jesus Christ! What a woman! But she is a little cracked. Really, really out there someplace. You'd never tell it looking at her, but she is completely nuts. Like this crap about me being in disguise. Where does she get this? Who the hell knows? Three nuns, indeed—three damned nuns. Why did she yell that out? What was in her mind? We were having sex! Why nuns? Still, that sounded pretty funny.

I've been horny since a boy. I used to play with myself a lot—in secret, of course. I used to play with myself so much that I got blisters, and not on my hands. On my hands I got calluses. I remember one summer where I did it like ten times a day. There was nothing else better to do. Summer is like that when you're home alone all day—alone with those glossy magazines and those dirty pictures.

I used to go down to Tyler's news store and ask What have you got behind the counter? And even though I was just a young lad back then, he'd show me the newest magazines, all sealed in plastic. They weren't ever out on display. They were far too much for that—too far out, so to speak. I'd probably buy about one a week. I hid them up in the rafters down in the cellar. No one ever found them. My friends hid their under their mattresses, and they always got found. Not mine. And when my folks were gone for the day, and I pretended to be sitting just watching television, I'd go down there and stuff my own hand. The air was all musty down there just like the way the air is thick and damp every time I'm with Christine. I smell those same smells and then I start to feel those same feelings. She takes me back. She's special that way. She makes me like a horny little boy all over again. It feels good, her musty house, and her shining milky tits. She's an old-fashioned girl that way. I really love her for that, in a way. I do. I love her. Even though I pay her through my nose, since time with her isn't cheap on my salary, I still love her. Except when she talks crazy talk like she did today.

Not that I love her in the way like I would if I wanted to get married and make a house together and have kids, and all that, but in some other way. Some other way that doesn't even have to do with the sex. Maybe it sounds sick, but Christine is so much younger than me that I think I love her like a daughter—I don't have any of my own. Not when we're having the sex though. That would be sick. She gets paid to give the sex and when she's giving the sex I really do think of her as a warm place to put my ego, or that is how I've heard it described. But outside of the sex, she's— she's like a daughter I've always wanted. That is why I worry about this whole thing. I worry both about myself, and about her. About myself in that I hope that I can step back and rationally look at this and say she's like a daughter to me that occasionally turns into an object for which I have nothing but sexual feelings; keeping both of those feelings as far apart as they should be, when at times she's not much different than my own stroking hand.

And I don't love my hand.

But I do love myself.

Anyway, never mind all that—between those times, when I love her, and when I need her, I worry that she is going every bit a little more crazy—like tonight with all her talk about me being in all those different disguises. It makes me wonder, is she joking around with me, play acting a part, or is she serious? If she is serious, that's not a good thing. She's not only at the edge; she's over the edge if she's being serious.

She has told me she was in the hospital for many years and that she never went to school. Though after I pushed her, she did admit to thinking about getting her GED and maybe getting a real job someplace. She told me that her mother and she have been given two weeks to clean up the place and then the city is going to come in and do an inspection. She fully expects, she says, for them to fail the inspection and that she and her Mother will be forced out onto the streets. Hearing that makes me wish that I was single again—as much as having the wife from hell makes me wish I was still single. Anyway, I could take Christine and her mother in, and give them rooms in my place. My house is big enough and I make enough money to cover the whole place. But, let's be honest,

I'd have to get Christine to give up her sex business and get a real job. Because every time she would bring a different man into my house it would cut up my heart—because I'd be thinking of her as my daughter during those times! I can see myself screaming Get off of my God-damned daughter! If you've have to get something done, go home and use your God-damned hand and save your three hundred dollars you troll faced ass fuck! Yes that's what she charges me for an evening with her—from about seven thirty to midnight, or whatever, give or take a half hour extra. And at that price, I can do her as many times as I want. But she allows straight sex only. She doesn't and wouldn't do anything weird. Not my girl. Not my daughter. If she did move in with me she wouldn't be able to do any of that at all. She would have to get a real job. Not that I can picture it—her with a real job, not with those hips, and those tits—every where she'd go, everyone would want to fuck her. But that's what it would have to be. Honestly when I'm not with Christine I picture her lying in the bed under the sheet with the back of her hand on her forehead, looking for me. Looking for me with those big eyes. She's like a big child in there, with those eyes. Maybe this all sounds like sick thinking. But there's no harm in it as long as I keep it to myself—in my mind. But the way I think of her in between—maybe I should be home using my hand. Maybe I should think of myself the way I would think of the other guys. Maybe I should put her on a pedestal, like you would a daughter; not a wife, but a daughter. Maybe I should go and lube up my hand and go to it and think of some other whore, or think of those glossy magazine girls, stuck between the pages, hidden up in the rafters under the floor boards. I wish, I wish—I wish I still had those magazines.

I used to go down to the creek, get under the trestle there and climb up into the trusses and lay the magazines on the steel and jack my dick off there. I like to do it there alone in the dark. It was my favorite place—until the day that Johnson kid, from my class, came walking under the trestle and he saw me. He stopped and looked up.

What are you doing? he said plainly. He didn't laugh or even smile. He just asked me while I crouched there in the trusses above him with my big fat penis in my hand.

What does it look like I'm doing? I said—now get out of here—and don't dare tell anybody you saw me here.

Okay, Johnson said without emotion. He put his hands in his pockets, walked out from under the bridge and was gone.

He was in the same class with me in grammar school. But it was funny—I never felt embarrassed about it. I thought, I'm doing this, and I don't care if you saw me. But I cared if others knew about it. So that's why I said to him to keep his mouth shut. It didn't matter that a little piece of dirt like him saw me, no—it mattered what the others think.

Not him.

He was a zero.

What kind of fucking name is Johnson? I mean really.

I often wonder where he is today and if he remembers that moment when our eyes locked while I sat there above him with my penis hard in my hand, my juice dripping down on top of him. If he's still alive, we are both old now, walled apart by time and space, but yet in this one way, we are still so near. I can see him like it was happening now—looking up at me there from under the bridge, the trusses like bars on a cage, looking up at me there, my penis hard in my hand, furiously jacking the foreskin back and forth, like a monkey in a zoo.

At school my friends Barry and Ronnie used to bully Johnson; they thought he was a runt. They used to bully Johnson, and they always wanted me to participate, but I never did, I stood back. From that moment over the creek, there was a always a secret bond between me and Johnson that has lasted all those years and I'll tell you the truth, I hope he remembers that moment under the bridge, that moment when I could feel the heat of my shame, pride and lust all flush across my face with him watching.

His face stared all blank. All fascinated somehow.

He looked, and all of a sudden he was gone.

When I was done masturbating, and I had come, my semen dropping to the creek bed below, I climbed down from the trusses and looked up and down the path along the creek hoping that he was still there, and that he had watched it all, but he wasn't there. I went around by the dam, and he wasn't there either. I walked back under and through the trestle and up on the path up toward home, and he wasn't on that side either. I often wonder if he's anywhere now. I wonder if he is alive or if he's dead. If he's dead I could forget about that afternoon—and I could finally abandon my little fantasy that comes into my head when I'm having sex with Christine.

Up here, I sit; I'm up in the trusses. Christine is there with me. We are having sex, I'm fucking her, going at her pussy hard, and I am holding her tight to keep her from falling into the creek below. We are not alone. Johnson knowingly walks up under the bridge—he has a girl with him—a girl with big glasses and blonde hair all the way down her back. They are holding hands. He looks up at me—actually, they both look up at us, and Christine and I look down at them. And then, as if prearranged, they climb into the trusses on the other side and start doing it too, so that we are all there under the bridge doing it together.

Together is how I love to do it.

Always have.

Together.

I am not some curled up alone creature stuck up in the under-corner of a dirty bridge, rotting away on the inside—rotting, rotting, only to be discovered by an innocent child walking by below—no, we are all up there together.

When I think about it, it makes it like the first time I came. I closed my eyes. I lie under the sheets. I see a boy up in the trusses. He looked at me and he said, don't tell a soul. I don't tell a soul. I moved my hand like he moved his hands over his penis because it looked cool. He was the cool kid in school. He was the big one— the biggest one, a bully to some even.

Under the covers, all at once, the room slid away and I was showered in a white fluid that shuddered over me and something big happened—I was all goosebumps and thrills. Overheated, I kicked the sheet to the bottom of the bed and I fell asleep. Is this why he was in the trusses? Is this why we are in the trusses? And when I awoke, there was Christine lying next to me asleep—a gleam in some man's eye.

She told me once, when we were done fucking, that her Father's name had been Martin, but that he had died in a truck accident. And that her mother had fallen apart after his death and that was when the place went to hell. When she got out of the hospital and came home the place was such a mess of garbage stacked to the ceilings all around, that there was nothing that she could do about it. And now she tells me that they are going to get thrown out. I know I should offer to help Christine clean up her mother's mess. I should offer this to her, the next time I am there and we are in between our fucking, I will offer it to her. But I know I won't actually help her clean up. It's easier to stay up in the trusses without anybody with me but my hand—abandoned and alone. Just like Christine. Together we are like brother and sister, Like father and child—lover and lover; each alone.

But together with her, I want to help her and her Mom. I really do. Really.

I have no friends. I go to work every day and I see people there, but they are not my friends. They are just paper cutouts moving around our make-believe, mock up of an office where I work. My boss, telling me how well I'm doing, is a paper cutout. I walk the streets, I go to the store, stop to have a cup of coffee, the paper cutouts standing all around me with their fake smiles and their glinty eyes with their cups of coffee, their silent talk and their perfectly coiffed hair. Alone, I make my way through them, I always do. I go down to the creek and I climb back into the trusses, leaving my coffee on the creek bed below. And she is there, she is always there, blood and bone, flesh, and eyes, and hair, up in her little room, with her chair, and vanity in the corner, and her bed, into which she beckons me, in the center of it all.

How are you Serdon? she always says—another week for you, another two hundred dollars for me, she jokes.

Yes, Christine loves a good joke.

This is one of the big reasons I love her.

So, I hand the money over. Right up front. Two hundred dollars a week for Christine; that's almost a thousand a month. She gives me a discount. She tells me that she usually charges three. And then she is there with me up under the bridge; we're tucked there like nesting birds. Nesting birds to be discovered by boys. Hopefully the right boy; hopefully not a boy who will get a stick and reach up and poke down our little nest. Hopefully the right boy. A boy that will ask us, what we're doing?

Nesting, I say, clutching Christine close to me.

Nesting?

Yes nesting. So move on boy.

It's then that I realize that this kid was not a cardboard cutout like all the others and it comes to me that there is still hope for the world. There are still some out there, like me and Christine who climb up and nest, and others, like the boy, who looks up wondering what's going on. There are still some out there with flesh blood and bone, wondering about the world.

Did you see that boy? said Christine, lying in my arms.

Yes. I've seen him before. That's Johnson. He's everywhere, he goes around everywhere.

Oh yeah? Huh. He looks so young—

But then Christine is gone, the trestle fades away, and I am driving the car home. I press the garage door remote that's balky, and doesn't always open the door. I'm going to have to get out of the car to open the garage door. All of a sudden someone's waving in the window; my wife Marnie; shit. I grip for the trusses, but they're not there anymore. I grab for Christine, but she too is gone. The car sits there, and it starts raining. I can no longer see Marnie waving for me to come from the window. Though midnight's long gone

I decide to wait until the rain has stopped. I decide to stay sitting alone in the car until the rain is stopped, there's no sense getting all wet. I sit there while it pours, pours, and pours—knowing Marnie's given up and left her place at the window a long time ago.

10 – The Inspection

THE DAY ARRIVED FOR THE INSPECTION. CHRISTINE CAME OUT ONTO the front porch to wait for the inspector to come at nine in the morning. That was what time the notice had said someone would show up. Christine and Thelma had decided that Thelma could not bear greeting the man. He was the man who would be taking her house away. Christine! Christine—

Christine raised her head from her hands and heard Thelma crying out, and rushed into the house to find her. As she tightened her robe around her, she glanced out; the world still dark; the world was going even darker this day, she thought to herself. She rushed her mother's room, stumbling through the trash. Turning on the lights, she saw Thelma lying on her bed, clutching at her throat with her eyes closed, crying out.

Christine! Christine—

Christine rushed to her and sat on the bed and shook her by the shoulder.

Mom, she breathed. Mom wake up you're dreaming—Mom—

Thelma's eyes opened and they melted into pools of blue liquid at the sight of her daughter. She squeezed Christine's hand, hard.

Christine, she said hoarsely—I—I was dreaming. It was awful they were tearing down the house, they didn't bother to inspect or anything, they just came with big dirty yellow machines and started tearing the place down—that's not what they're going to do today is it is it—

No, breathed Christine. They're just looking at the place today. They're just looking, Mom.

Today's the day right isn't it? The day we have to —oh my God—get out?

No Mom. They're just looking at the place today. We talked about this. We talked about this yesterday. They're just coming to look.

The old woman's eyes bugged and she half sat up and said Where will we go when they make us get out? You know they're going to make us get out. You know that right?

Christine gently urged her mother back down.

No, not today, Mom. Not today. There's just a man coming to look. To look and talk.

Look and talk?

Yes.

That's all they're going to do—they're not going to tell us to get out?

Unseen, the bugs swarmed beneath the trash, stirred up by all the excitement.

Yes, that's all they're going to do today. Don't worry Mom. Please don't worry.

All right.

Christine sat with her Mother a while and Thelma's eyes closed back down and she fell lightly back asleep. The room around the bed was all full of boxes and bags piled high. Spider webs stretched across the window and hung from the blades of the motionless ceiling fan above. Christine sat holding her mother's hand and wondered if this was the very bed where she was conceived in. It probably was, she decided. Things would have looked so different that day so long ago. In the dark of the night, they had laid there, her mother and her father; in the dark of the night, before all this, they had lain right here making a little Christine.

What shall we name the baby if he's a boy, Thelma? Martin might have asked.

They'd sat on the bed together and talked into the night.

I don't know, Thelma might have responded. She was so young, and her eyes so bright.

But if she's a girl, we will name her Christine, she certainly replied.

Why Christine, Martin had said.

She came to me in a dream. I saw her. Her name is Christine. She's going to be a girl, I know that for sure.

How can you know that for sure?

I just do. I said—I saw it in a dream.

Now her mother lay asleep, Christine holding her hand, her chest moving with her light breathing. Gently Christine opened her hand and let her mother's hand lie on the blanket. She will sleep now, thought Christine. But she is right to ask. Where will we go when they put us out? Where will we go, and how will we live when they take our home away from us?

With this question in her mind Christine rose and backed out from her parent's bedroom and let her mother continue sleeping. She closed Thelma's door and stood in the dark hall. As long as it stayed dark they could not see the trash. As long as it stayed dark outside, no one in the town could see the house. And as long as no one could see the house, they were safe.

The bugs beneath the boxes and bags in the silent room stilled.

Christine turned and felt her way back to the stairs and went back to her room and lay on the bed. A tear rolled down her cheek but she was not crying. She wiped it away not sure she knew what it was there for. She did not feel sad. Gradually light began to filter in through the window and she lay there with an empty mind kneading her hands in the blanket and all at once Leandra was there next to her again. She stepped out of the shadows and sat on the vanity chair and she spoke to Christine.

So where are we going to live honey?

She picked up Christine's hair brush and began brushing her long brown hair.

I don't know, muttered Christine. I suppose I should start looking into that. They're bound to put us out after they see the place.

How long after you fail the inspection do you have before you have to get out?

I don't know.

Ask the inspector today how long you have. But how will you find another place to live? How do you do that? Leandra asked.

I don't really know. I guess we will cross that bridge when we come to it.

Yes I guess, Leandra said stroking her hair.

The dawn came up, the unseen jungle surrounding the house dissolved up into the morning glow, and Christine rose and went downstairs, finding that while she had been up in her room Thelma had risen and sat now in the kitchen, eating burnt toast at a small space she had cleared on the table. As Christine came into the kitchen Thelma pointed to the space where her toast lay.

Look I cleared that space on the table—make sure you show the man how I cleared some space on the table. That's cleaning up right? Isn't that cleaning up?

Yes it is. I will show them, Mom. Hey listen, let me do the talking today okay? Don't say anything to the inspector.

Why not?

Because I know what to say and we don't want to confuse them.

You think I would confuse them?

No—no, not that. It's just it will be best if only one of us talks. Suddenly Christine's face lit up, a joke coming up behind her.

Hey you know maybe I can charm the guy let him have a freebie upstairs that would make him happy; maybe if I do him, he will pass the inspection—or even freebies for life, that's it. I'll give him freebies for life if he passes us!

Thelma smiled slightly but her half closed eyes didn't.

Don't joke that way Christine, you know I don't like it when you joke that way.

Well—I like it, said Christine, chuckling. This keeps us going Mom, this gets us through the days—a little funny stuff, you know, and some kindness from strangers.

Mother smiled chewing. They looked into each other's eyes. A bubble of love came around them, that no one could enter.

This is my mother, thought Christine. And no matter what happens, I will protect her.

This is why I was sent to her.

Sent to her, and my Father, up in that room on that bed.

Breakfast time came and went. Christine, as usual, had nothing. She went up to her room, took off her robe, got dressed, and ended up back outside, on the porch waiting, for the inspector to come. The trash on the lawn spread out stinking before her, but she didn't see it. She just saw the path through the trash that her Johns came through and that the inspector would come through when he got there.

See, she thought—see, the way is clear, you can get in—just like all the other men. So what if you can't see the lawn. Who needs lawns anyways?

Leandra smiled waiting next to her as the rising sun cut across the yard and finally, at nine, a small yellow truck came up and pulled before the house. BOROUGH OF DESHLER it said on the side door, a figure sitting behind the wheel. As she rose, Christine craned to see who it was.

Freebies for life, she thought.

And Leandra chuckled You wouldn't dare.

Freebies for life to pass us this inspection?—sure I would, she smiled

The truck door opened and a tall woman with blonde hair got out wearing a yellow hard hat, holding a clipboard. She stood looking at the clipboard and glanced up at the house and back down at the clipboard and she came toward the gate.

Damn it, no freebies, thought Christine, watching.

Don't say no to anything, Christine, whispered Leandra—that's what you tell your boys—

As Christine smiled for an instant, the woman kept her head down as she came up through the path and finally stood at the bottom of the porch steps.

Hello Ma'am, she said, looking up—are you Thelma Zidar?

No, Christine replied. That's my mother. She's inside. I'm Christine Zidar.

The woman scanned the yard and wrote something quickly on the clipboard and looked at Christine and said quizzically, did you know we were coming to inspect today?

Yes we did—

For life, chuckled Leandra at her side—remember you said it—Freebies for life—

The woman gained the first step and said from her lightly freckled face, It doesn't look like you cleaned up very much out here. What about inside? Did you clean up the insides?

I—uh—a little, stuttered Christine.

Well let's go inside and see, said the inspector. My name is Diana.

The women shook hands. Diana, thought Christine—isn't that the Goddess of the hunt? Or the Goddess of something—Leandra, is Diana the Goddess of the hunt?

Yes, she's the Goddess of the hunt and wild animals, and later at night she's the Goddess of the moon, said Leandra silently.

Jungle and moon. Moon and jungle. Funny, funny, Something in her knows, but—

Diana's tilted her head as she held Christine's hand.

Are you all right Miss Zidar? It looks a little like you might be coming down with something—

—of the hunt wild animals and the moon, she thought—fighting off the thoughts, Christine blurted Oh. No! I'm all right. Just sleepy I guess, I've been up all morning waiting for the inspection, she explained as they parted hands.

Good, said Diana. Let's go inside then.

They stepped around the boxes stacked on the porch and the old rusted refrigerator by the door and Christine opened the front door which once had had beautiful stained glass but now had rain stained cardboard duct taped over it, and ushered Diana in. With some effort, the door pushed open. Inside, the foyer was dark with clutter to the ceiling on both sides of the door.

Is this safe? asked Diana.

Oh yes, said Christine. It is all safe.

Through the path leading up to the kitchen, in came Thelma, a cup of coffee in her hand.

Hello, she said. You must be the inspector. I'm Thelma Zidar. This is my house, welcome.

Hello, good to meet you, said the woman, extending a hand. I'm Diana.

They shook hands and Diana wasted no time getting down to business.

Your daughter says you knew you were being inspected today. From what I can see in the yard and in this foyer, you haven't cleaned much up—

Martin stood in the corner of the hall watching from next to a pile of boxes, but he said nothing.

Goddess of the hunt, Goddess of wild animals and of the moon, said Leandra. You got to be kidding me—

We've done the best we can, said Thelma.

But—look at all this, said the inspector, waving a hand.

Like I said, said Thelma in a hard voice. This is my house—

Christine touched Thelma's arm.

Mom—remember what we said this morning. I—

I know you said you would do all the talking but this is my house and if she doesn't like my house well, I like my house just fine—

Martin took one step forward.

Mom! said Christine, squeezing her mother's arm. Thelma quieted down.

Which of you two work? asked Diana. Who's the breadwinner in this house?

Martin was a contractor when he was alive—my husband Martin that is—

Martin watched silently from the corner.

Mother gets some money from her husband's social security and she gets a small pension, said Christine. But, I'm the bread-winner—

Leandra smiled, She's going to have to hear it she just had to know—

What do you do? said Diana.

I'm a consultant, snapped Christine. I run my own consulting business out of the house.

Leandra laughed so hard, that it made Christine crack a smile.

Consulting? said Diana, as she wrote it on her clipboard. What kind of consulting is it?

Martin stood listening, glowering.

Diana, listen, said Christine gently but in a slightly raised voice. I don't really see what these questions have to do with what you're here for today.

Diana tipped back her clipboard.

I'm just trying to see if you've also got a zoning violation by running a business out of your house in this residential area—what kind of consulting do you do?

Counseling, said Christine. I do—marriage counseling.

Leandra could not stop laughing; and Christine didn't know where she got what she said but it sounded all right to her. Just pulled it from the air, just from the air—and, it made sense too. What she did was, in a twisted way, a kind of marriage counseling. Thelma just stood there blank-faced, listening As Diana wrote in her notebook and spoke.

It's against the law to run a business from your house in this neighborhood. I have to look into this further—but I believe marriage counseling might be all right.

And she wrote some more onto her clipboard.

You know, said Christine—what happens today is all academic anyway—we've filed for an extension—

You only get ten extensions, said Diana. According to the records I have here, you've already had your ten.

She looked up from the clipboard, pencil poised. The door was behind her. The door the officer came to over twenty years ago. The door that Thelma opened and it was all sunshine and green grass and leaves behind the officer, all neat and clean, when he said it.

Is Martin Zidar your husband?

Yes, said Thelma.

I'm afraid to inform you that he's died in a truck accident.

What?

A truck accident—he's died—

All that happened twenty years ago in the space just behind this inspector and that was when the house started to fill up, almost on its own and that was when Christine started to go downhill at that lousy day care center and Thelma got a job at the stinking dress factory and that all happened, right there behind this inspector, this Diana, Goddess of the hunt and the wild animals and of the moon too; jungle and moon, moon and jungle.

Beautiful things, moon and jungle. Words came out of them up in Christine.

We filed for another extension last week, said Christine. They didn't say anything about a limit of ten.

Oh I bet they did, said Diana. But let's not argue about that now. I'm here to inspect—and from what I can see, you've made no effort to clean up—at least not the yard. At least not this part of the house either. Look. We're walking on trash—and it stinks—

And the police officer who told her Martin died just left, leaving Thelma alone and that was what always happened with people like this they came and went and left you alone and you end up in a Goddamned dress factory at a stinking lousy sewing machine all black and greasy like the inside of this Diana's mind, all black and greasy—the house stinks who's she to say the house stinks—she doesn't know the history she doesn't know what went on after the officer left, what they've gone through what—

I need to see the rest of the house, said Diana.

They went into the kitchen and squeezed around the stacked trash and shuffled over the old wrappers and crushed boxes and papers and other trash underfoot, causing the buglife beneath to stir and scurry, until at last they stood in the doorway. The room was a cascading jumbled multicolored sloping mass burying the sink, the stove with its built in oven and all and there was were the two chairs, one for Thelma and one for Christine, tilting on the garbage, hovering beside the table.

My God, said Diana—and they stood there as Thelma over twenty years younger cleaned a turkey in the spotless sink and the room was all neat, clean and wholesome smelling. The calendar neatly pinned to the wall said that it was November and that it was time to cook the Thanksgiving meal for Martin and little Christine. Thelma turned on the cold water and it washed over the thawed turkey, as she worked on the counter cutting vegetables, in her flowered apron, with a smile on her face—

There are pictures I can prove it somewhere in here someplace there are pictures—

This place is a mess, said Diana—you haven't done a thing here either.

For six hours, she had timed the cooking to the weight of the bird, the smell of the roasting turkey filled the clean house, the giblets simmering and Thelma fixing the gravy, her hair brown not grey and her steps solid and sure, not weak and halting as Martin pushed his way in past the trio in the doorway and went up to his wife, hugged her from behind and turning her towards him, he kissed her, her nose dusted with flour. Christine and Thelma and Diana stood there unseeing and forgotten what had once been, in the place of the slanting mounds of trash and the stinking rotting food sloping to the chairs each facing a cleared-off segment of the unseen kitchen table and Diana stepped into the room furiously writing on her clipboard, kicking garbage aside.

This is bad, really bad—what's through this door?

The dining room, said Christine.

Diana stood in the door—blocked completely with boxes full of rags, tin cans, and grease stained trash, the door impossible to open and the room impossible to enter. The dining room itself was buried tight; packed full on the inside, the table was set with the turkey and Thelma was serving the food. Martin was there in his new glasses and baby Christine was in her high chair, the one with the elephants on it. They were having Thanksgiving dinner and you could still see the crystal chandelier engulfed by bags of trash on all sides. In the summers they had hamburgers and potato salad that Thelma had made from scratch, but now the room was sealed tight, packed full. Elephants, elephants—yes somewhere there are pictures to prove it yes—

Diana said, I quite frankly don't think I've ever seen anything this bad; but Thelma and Christine knew she couldn't see past the garbage like they could; and that it was only after Martin died that it all started to fill up like that. It was fine before, all fine before, it was important for Diana to see that, but she couldn't see that so she just put down on her clipboard what she could see and they knew that was what they were going to be judged on.

Goo, little Christine had said, kneading her first hamburger. Goo. Goo Goo—

Diana turned to Thelma and Christine.

Okay, she said—I'd like to think I have seen enough, but I need to see the whole house—where's the living room?

Through here, said Christine, as she led the way through the door and to the left. And there they were—young Thelma, Martin, in chairs watching TV and little Christine on the floor playing dolls, with garish but at that time fashionable wallpaper all around, but now buried in a mass of boxes and bags of books, pots and pans, piled up around them, drowning them as sure as water would drown them. The sea of trash heaving like swells in the ocean and they, Thelma, Martin and their young Christine, were under there; frozen in time, like in Pompeii, how it got buried under the ash, bodies sitting peacefully in unseen chairs. Then Martin had died and Thelma had came into the living room holding little Christine and she had thrown herself into the chair and she had cried; and cried, and the house had started to fill up around her in that chair because the chair had to be buried so that she wouldn't see it every day, see herself crying there.

Thelma was trying to tell Diana, who was writing all over her clipboard, there's a beautiful hardwood floor under there—there's a beautiful hardwood floor, you ought to see it.

Mom, mom, breathed Christine, placing a hand gently on the old woman. Mom—

That's nice, said Diana, finishing up her writing. Then she clapped the clipboard under her arm and looked at Christine and said Upstairs now please? We have to go upstairs—

Christine kicked aside bags of trash and the piles of litter and the three headed for the darkened stairs clogged with boxes fallen down and bags and boxes still stacked on top of each other. They struggled up the stairs.

God! What the hell is all this! shouted Diana suddenly—these stairs are blocked. They're a fire hazard, a safety hazard. What if the rescue squad needed to get up here? They'd never make it. God almighty!

While Diana went on and on, increasingly amazed, Christine's Johns started pushing past them, rushing to get to her room before they did, knocking boxes and bags over in their rush to see her. They all loved Christine, and they all had rushed up these stairs many times before.

See? Thought Christine—my men have no trouble with these stairs why are you having trouble you Diana you why—

But Diana couldn't see any men, she could just see the trash moving, threatening to tumble, all threatening to come down in a heap. Only Leandra and Christine could see the Johns disappearing one by one into the dark up in the stairhead. When Diana got to the top of the stairs onto the landing and into the hallway, she saw that it too was packed with bound up papers stacked on either side and there was a door to the right. Diana led the way inside. The room was filled from top to bottom like the dining room and in this room Martin had kept his lovebirds. When he was alive he had taken their eggs and brought them down to the kitchen and broken them open, calling out to his wife in the living room saying There's fertile eggs here—there's blood in the eggs. And mother came and looked and they were like little hen's eggs with a yellow yolk in the center, and a clear jelly around it and there was a streak of blood in them; there always was a streak of blood in them and now they stood in the door of the love birds' room and the trash was packed in like it had been in the dining room but the cage was still in there, buried and the birds are still in there, buried and there were hundreds of thousands of eggs in there, buried for twenty years and some of the eggs had hatched; and there were baby birds starving in there, starving because no one can get in and feed them; Martin could have gotten in there to feed them but Martin was dead; the officer had said so, died in a truck accident. And the baby birds were starving—because of what the officer had said—

All at once Thelma nearly collapsed, and Christine caught her.

Christine snapped at Diana, Haven't you seen enough? My mother is suffering.

Diana said, we're almost done. almost—what's over there?

My room, said Christine—my room.

The hall was dark. The light above was burned out but when the bedroom door opened, somehow light came from the room;

clean pure light that made Christine say Come on. Come in. Look, and see—and in a minute they were in her room and Thelma was sitting in the vanity chair and the room stretched around them, spotless and shining.

Wow, what a difference from the rest of the house, said Diana— why is this room so different from the rest of the house—this room is perfect. It even smells good.

The wide bed lay gleaming white in front of them and for the twenty years that Christine had been in the hospital Thelma had kept the room perfectly clean, dusting, polishing, changing the sheets weekly even though no one was sleeping there, and there she was in there now, all bent over, rushing around the room, dusting, cleaning, sweeping, polishing—got to keep the room ready for my little Christine, she sang. Someday she will come back. Someday they'll let her go, and they'll let her come home and this will be her room—

Thelma raised her head.

I am proud of this room, she said to Diana. This room is perfect just like my daughter here.

Leandra smiled and poked Christine in the ribs and Christine flinched and Diana noticed and said, what's wrong and Christine frowned at Leandra and said, nothing, just an itch—I've got an itch. The Johns writhed on the bed—marriage counseling. Leandra laughed, Christine smiled. Marriage counseling! Writhing there on the bed!

And can I see your office space? said Diana.

Office space?

Yes. You said you do counseling.

Oh—here—this is my office.

The wide bed beckoned as always.

But this is just a bedroom.

We sit on the bed.

Oh.

Diana wrote that on the clipboard.

Down at the police station, they knew that Christine was a whore. When she started out, she got caught trying to pick up an undercover policeman downtown and they brought her in and she said, No—I'm just friendly. I was looking for a friend—and the cops all looked at each other and they laughed—they laughed and laughed and laughed and they still remember her down there, even though they let her go that day with a ticket and a slap on the wrist and Thelma never knew about it because Christine never told her, knowing that she would have been mortified.

Still, the inspection wore on and on, and they went up into the clogged attic and then down into the more-than clogged basement and into the trash filled garage and then all at once they stood in the yard with Diana writing on to the clipboard, silence rising around them as the nighttime jungle lay down just below their feet, sleeping, and they waited until finally Diana let the clipboard down and raised her face and spoke.

I'm afraid you have failed the inspection Ma'am, she said to the women. I'm afraid you have failed pretty badly.

No, said Christine, waving a hand—we have not failed. This inspection should never have happened. We've got an appeal in. This inspection was supposed to happen a month from now; plenty of time to clean up please, we just needed a little more time to clean the place up—

Diana raised a hand at the house.

You see how the house is, said Diana. You have appealed ten times. Ten times is the limit and you see how the house is—

But they said they would consider one more appeal.

Diana waved aside the words and said Now you will hear next from the town as to how we are going to proceed, now that you have failed—

Now that you have failed.

Now that you have failed.

Now that you have failed—

And Christine saw the trash in the yard part and there were the bodies of Everest all around and somehow they were all at the peak draped on the summit. The snow field stretched all around them with the dead all around her and Leandra—

Do you have any other questions for me before I go? asked Diana, tilting her hard hat back slightly.

—no she is here standing here on the mountain with the words drifting across the snow, what did she say? Who is this woman? What did she say? Who is she to say anything in my yard? Get out of here get out of my yard—

No, said Christine.

—get out of my yard—

—get out of damned my yard—

—my God damned yard—

Diana shrugged and went to her car and drove away without saying goodbye

—no manners no manners.

Well I guess we told her, said Christine to Leandra.

What dear, said Thelma staring around at all the bodies—what did you say.

Nothing, nothing.

Nothing at all, my love.

The wild nighttime jungle slept on beneath them.

And Martin watched unseen in the front door up past the porch; the door around him all full of his dead gone darkness.

11 - Intermetamorphosis

BARRY REINHARDT LAY IN CHRISTINE'S BED, HANDS FOLDED ACROSS his tummy, Christine sitting naked at the vanity brushing out her hair and listening.

You know, Christine, said Barry—if only I had married you instead of my wife—if only I had known you before—years ago. What a pair we would have made, what a pair. Don't you think so Christine?

Oh sure—

Yeah, he smiled—married in a nice house with a bunch of little Barrys and Christines running around—what do you think Christine?

He lay with his hands behind his head and he chewed his tongue; a habit of his. Christine looked at herself in the mirror and thought What a hypocrite this guy is. He's not really Barry. He's Bud down from that greasy, old smelly gas station. He's that big fat guy with the porous nose all speckled with blackheads who stares me up and down whenever I go in to pay. But I'm going to play along. I can't let him know I know who he really is. Why should I?

The brush moved. Up, down, up, down.

The phony in the bed went on talking.

What do you think, Christine? Why you so quiet?

No, Christine decided, she would say nothing. She knew. That was enough. No point in giving anything away about herself to this porous-nosed lecherous stranger. But she could play with him, yes, that's what she would do. She put the brush down and turned around.

So how do you like running a gas station? What's it like?

Oh—I don't run the gas station. Bud does. I just work on cars and pump gas. Why would I want the headaches of running a gas station? Bud can have it—

She would say it she would—

You know you shouldn't lie to me, she said, narrow-eyed—because I know.

What? said Barry—what do you know—

You know, she said. You know very well. Tell me who you really are.

She looked at him and fear crossed his face momentarily before fading.

I—I'm Barry Reinhardt, he said—you know who I really am.

—okay let it out—let it all out—

You do look like Barry. That's a really good disguise, she smiled. Huh?

I know you're really Bud from the gas station—so how are you doing Bud?

Her smile dawned and became sunny all over her whole face.

Barry said, Come on, cut it out Christine—it's spooky. Come here—

He said as he patted the bed beside him.

—come here and let me snap you out of it.

She sat there naked swinging the brush, her hair hanging down.

Did you know that this house is about to be condemned out

from under me and my Mom—and you think you got it hard running a damned gas station? How would you like to be in me and Mom's shoes?

Well—I don't know, said Barry, confused—maybe you and your Mom should clean the place out.

She pointed at him.

You know, you're just like a man to say a stupid thing like that!

What?

She leaned back smiling, Never mind—so tell me—how do you do it? Maybe I could do it too—but you men all do the craziest things and won't let me in on what you are doing or how to do it—

Doing what? he asked quizzically.

Right Bud, she said—how do you switch places with Barry—do you two do it a lot? Could you switch back right now? Is it somehow sexy—sure I bet it's sexy somehow—sexy is what everything has to be for you men—but I really want to talk to Barry, not an old ugly thing like you—you know that's what you are, right? An old ugly thing, hiding inside Barry. Come on, be Barry—

He patted the bed, Come here Christine—

But I don't want to have sex with you, Bud. I want to be with Barry.

Barry opened his arms. He would play her game. Christine and her games—

Okay, he said snapping his fingers—here—now I'm Barry. Barry's back, okay? Now will you come here and lay down by me?

She nearly laughed out loud, Prove to me you're Barry, said Christine.

How the hell am I supposed to do that?

I don't know. Tell me something only Barry would know.

Like what? I have Bud over all the time—he knows my wife and kids, he's been at my house—

Tell me how many times you masturbate a day.

What? I don't masturbate, you know that, I've told you that—

You're lying—you're not Barry—but seeing as I got your money. I'll do you and pretend you're Barry. It's only a body after all, after you get into it; deep into it, it's only just a body, and you men all look act and feel pretty much the same in the dark.

And she went to him and she did him, and afterward they lay intertwined together.

You know you are just like Barry, Bud. Every part of you is just like him. How do you guys do it?

Oh—it isn't easy, he said as he rolled his eyes toward the ceiling. She was warm in his arms. She could say whatever crazy thing she wanted—she was his Christine, and she was sweet and warm in his arms.

You know, said Christine dreamily—I could drive down to the gas station and ask Barry something that only he would know. You know I could.

He's not at the gas station in the night—hey Christine, tell me. Are you on the level? Do you really believe I'm Bud?

I do.

Why?

Leandra smiled and moved her hand along Barry's penis.

I—I don't know. I just know.

Oh, Christine, that feels so good—keep doing that—

What?

Your hand—keep moving your hand back and forth, just like that—

How do you know you're not doing that with your own hand, she said—I'm not doing anything with my hand.

Because I have my hands right here, he said as he pulled his hands out from behind his head. Look! Oh my God, Christine! Oh—

Suddenly she let go his penis, sprang from the bed, and hunched over the edge and laughed. She held up her hands to her face, they were covered in semen.

Gross, said Christine. You men are so damned gross.

What's gross about it, said Barry.

I—uh—what's on my fucking hand—I need to go wash my hands.

What?

I need to.

Christine went into her bathroom and closed the door and washed her hands as Leandra looked over her shoulder in the mirror.

What did you do that for? said Christine. You had my hand you moved my hand thank God he didn't see you. You made him come all over me.

I did it for a joke. Oh come one, it was funny—you thought it was funny.

Oh funny?—it was gross. My hand—

This is my hand not yours.

No this is mine.

Mine.

Mine.

Gross.

She looked down from Leandra and washed her hands and slipped on the bathrobe hanging from a peg and went back in to Barry.

Who were you talking to in there Christine? asked Barry.

Nobody, said Christine. She sat back on the vanity chair and resumed brushing her hair.

Don't do that anymore okay?

Do what? said Barry.

Slime my hand like that. Your slime is very gross.

But—it was your fault—you were the one rubbing me, besides it's not like you don't know what happens to me when I get aroused—it happens every time we have sex. Don't you get slimed all the time?

You're disgusting. Let's not talk about it any more.

Oh. Okay. But you were the one brought it up—

No more talk okay, she said in a hard voice.

Okay. Come here, Christine.

Why?

I'm ready to go again.

She brushed harder.

We just did it twice, Bud. That's the deal.

She turned back to the mirror and saw his body lying on the bed all white and lumpy and round like some beat-up melon.

Leandra was standing there next to her and she put her arm around Christine's shoulder.

We should go away, said Leandra. I know I got you into this, but I think you should stop doing this stuff and we should go away somewhere.

We can't, answered Christine. There's mother—

What are you talking to yourself in the mirror for, called out Barry from the bed.

She turned her heads.

Never mind Bud, this is none of your business. Just go to sleep. Take a nap. Or do something. You must be tired. I need to talk to myself, as you put it. I need to talk to myself the same way there's things you need to do to yourself. It keeps me healthy. Mentally healthy. Like you feel when you jack off.

Barry rolled over in the bed, tucked himself up into a fetal position.

Christine turned back to Leandra and they spoke in that instant, There, Leandra. Bud won't talk to us again. Where were we?

We were talking about your mother, said Leandra. What about when the house is condemned? What will become of her then?

I can't think about what will become of her then. I just hope it doesn't get condemned.

Yes but what if it does—

The walls of the bedroom expanded away and the ceiling shot up and they were in the clouds on the cold windblown peak of Mount Everest. The dead bodies, frozen, spread down from the peak. Leandra pulled Christine closer and spoke to comfort her; as she spoke, they warmed. She knew that she had to keep speaking for them to survive the cold, because in that frozen instant; inside her room, it was cold, bitterly cold.

What about all those poor people down there, Christine wondered—they thought they were going to be all right but then they got condemned by the ice and the snow and the wind and the cold and what did they do when they got condemned—they laid down and gave up and they came up here to heaven—

Heaven? This is heaven?

Yes heaven, they lay down and gave up and in their last moments they knew they were condemned the same way me and my mother might be condemned and they probably thought of God and of heaven—

Or maybe they just thought about how God-damned cold it was up here.

But instead the cold probably froze their thoughts, and after a while, before they actually died and I'm assuming that they did die at peace, so to speak, put to sleep by the cold, except for those who fell and are laying shattered in pieces, their deaths a little more frightening, and they lay where they fell, they're probably still laying there as we speak—what will freeze me and Thelma's thoughts when our house is condemned? Leandra, you tell me that you know so much, so tell me—would you please.

The ice and the snow and the cold that comes when you know the worst thing has happened and you don't know what you will do next, but you know that you will be frozen in the ice snow and cold. Like these people on this mountain must have known, even if only for a second, but many for much longer if they suffered to death.

The wind whipped up all around. Would it take the house? Was it strong enough to take the damned house and end their damned problems? Christine strained to hear, to hear—

So then you can know that they are at peace now, said Leandra. You could say that, yes, they ran into the worst thing that could happen so God froze them in the snow, the ice, the wind and cold and brought their quest of life to the end. Life is a quest you know. Life is a quest for happiness and freedom and all sorts of things. All these people here are happy and free because for them there is nothing left and in nothingness there is happiness and freedom. In the end, which is black calm, there are no more quests. When the quest is over, everything these people ever wanted is fulfilled. They are in their eternal sleep, and so the question becomes the same, like—where do you go when you sleep? Or when you die? What was there before you were alive is what there will be after you die—both places are the same. But you can't remember any of it—that's what makes you scared. When this house gets condemned, that is if this house gets condemned, which I'm sure it will, you will return to how it was before the house was here, that time that you can't remember any of. Like those bodies on the mountain. Their souls are just lying there in that place; not a bad place to be, much better than living. Just nothing. Not warm, not cold, not dark, not bright, but whatever was before. That's what's after, Christine. Like these bodies. Their souls are now at peace. No more thinking about quests, or inspections, or condemnations or death; that was all taken away from them by the freezing ice cold and the wind, way up here, taking their life. You know?

That's something to think about, Leandra, said Christine, looking around at the rocks blistering in the cold. But if we're lucky the appeal will take and we'll get Mom more time to clean up.

Christine, you know that won't happen. Face it. She had years of warnings. Ten warnings in total, this last one was her final one, the borough man told you that, the inspector lady told you that, besides, your mother will never clean this place up. There are too many bodies. She likes the house just the way it is. She wants to keep everything buried and frozen in time.

The top of the mountain got too cold even for Leandra's embrace—and so they returned to Christine's room. The house came back together around them and it was still there. The bed was still there and Bud was still there sleeping in the bed but when they came back Bud woke up.

Hey Christine. I dozed off, just a second—just a second mind you. How about you jump into the bed with me now? One last time before I go, I'm all rested up, he said with a wink.

No you've got to go now, said Christine. You got your money's worth—and next time be yourself, be Bud. But if you want to know, you are not as much fun as Barry—tell Barry I said that. I had very little fun tonight. You had it all. You know?

Yeah okay, whatever, said Barry—and he got off the bed and rummaged through his clothes hung on the chairback by the bed. Still, you're the greatest, Christine—a little weird maybe—but still the greatest.

Make sure Barry hears that, she said smiling, be sure to tell him. Barry tossed the three hundred dollars to Christine and she counted it and said that there's fifty dollars too much there.

A tip, he said. A tip for all the laughs—you thinking I was Bud. What a laugh. That's a real gas. You're a nut, Christine. A funny little sexy nut!

But you are Bud. Don't come back as Barry again. Or I will surely kick you dead in the balls and you won't be good for nothing.

Goodbye Christine.

Bye Bud—

Christine my love, the name is Barry. You little devil!

Bye Bud.

Whatever. Bye.

He went out the door and clattered down the stairs as he stumbled over some trash and gradually the sounds stopped and he must have gotten by Thelma and out the door. They heard the sounds of a car starting outside, revving up, and driving off.

Well here we are, just you and me, Leandra, said Christine.

Sure is. Let's take a shower. He was dirty.

He's a mechanic, said Christine.

I thought you said he was the owner?

Get into the shower.

The water came on them and Leandra melted away and Christine figured she'd give all Barry's money to her Mother this time. Thelma deserves it. It will lift her spirits and she needs a lift, thought Christine aloud, toweling. She stood in her wet feet, toweling herself vigorously, getting the filth of that dirty man off her. They were all filthy, all of them, she said to herself—but no two were the same. Sometimes it seemed like they were all the same—but now, all clean like she was, she though they were just like snowflakes—they were all different—and all beautiful, filthy and beautiful. But not for long periods at a time. A couple of hours at a time, at most, and mostly just for laughs. Like snowflakes too, they were icy and cold. Like the peaks of Mount Everest. Like the peak, the slopes—the bed felt good in the dark, all warm. After this day. Sending Barry on his way, imagine. Sending God-damned Barry on his fucking way.

She snuggled down deep into her bed and peeked out from under her covers to see that the peak around her was still all windswept. Windswept. And so would tomorrow and the tomorrow after that and the tomorrow after that would be.

Whatever day will we end up hearing what the town will do, she wondered, sighing gently gripping the sheets around her. Her eyes closed down as sleep filled her and it was all wonderful as before she was born.

There was nothing, she whispered. Wonderful nothing. Nothing, like death must actually be; nothing. For there is no God—there can't be a God—there can't be a God to let this happen, leaving all those bodies up on the slopes of Mount Everest, she thought. All those bodies just lying there in nothingness, knowing; a nothingness that if there was a God he would never allow to exist. As her eyes closed, the house full of trash was all around her room; and in it she felt cocooned. She felt cocooned and emptied like nothing, and wonderful.

12 – Mount Everest IV

NOW THAT I'M DRIVING HOME FROM CHRISTINE'S PLACE, I'M THINK-ing; I've got no beef with Christine Zidar. But, to be honest, I'm a little bit put off that she kept on saying I was really Bud from the gas station. She can't believe that. That's much too crazy. I mean it didn't matter because I got what I paid for anyway. Maybe I'm just a little bit insulted—me? Bud? But I can shake it off. I'm a big man. I can take it. Bud has had his gas station for over fifty years. And the other day he told me something great.

I'm going to hand the station down to you, Barry.

What?

After I go—I don't mean to retire mind you, that won't happen—I'll die with my boots on, you know, as they say. But when I am gone, it will all become yours.

It was great to hear that. Nearly knocked me down. My future will be made then. The station is great. All modernized and such. Bud has been good to me. So is everyone—I'm a big man all around town. I was even mentioned in that book that they put out about the town a while back. This little brunette writer came around and interviewed me for it. Cute, made me a little hard you know, but she was nothing like Christine though. Nobody's like Christine. If things had been different in a lot of ways, I would have chosen to marry Christine, issues and all. She spent all her life, up until thirty, in that hospital upstate, in some kind of coma they say.

What kind of coma were you in all those years? I asked her, one time when we were done fucking.

Oh, she said—it wasn't really a coma—a semi coma of some kind, I guess. I went in and out, here and there, you know what I mean?

Not really, I said.

She just smiled. I knew she was in the hospital all the way over in Omaha. They've got a criminally insane wing. I tease her about that when she gets to talking crazy. I'd tell her, they should take you back to the crazy house—you should be in the crazy house, they should have never left you out, and we'd laugh. And her eyes would sparkle and flash knowing that I was just joking and that I liked her being a bit crazy. But I wasn't in the mood for that today. Today, with all her Bud talk, I needed to get in, get off and get out. Got big places to be. Big places to be and big people to meet. The Mayor wants to see me for lunch. His secretary said it was about the school board. I think he wants to appoint me to it, I hear there's a vacancy. I got kids in the school. I and Marcia would like to see things go right for them. I hope this is really about the school board. I really really do.

Marcia? Oh we're in love, Marcia and I get along. But Christine does things that Marcia won't, like take her time, and stare into my eyes when she takes me inside her and there are other things that I can't do on my own. Still nothing beats a real woman, and both Christine and Marcia are real women in their own ways. And because Marcia doesn't know, I don't think there's any harm in it.

I'm only spending three hundred a week, give or take a fifty. But I make enough money so that it's not missed at home. Bud's got me overseeing ten mechanics so I don't even have to get my hands dirty anymore—though I do. I don't have to, but I do. I like to help out. Get in there with the guys, you know. Get rough, get dirty. Bond, so to speak. That's the mark of a good leader.

I do worry about Christine going off the deep end. Sometimes I think this in the back of my mind, especially after some of the crazier things that she's told me, and had me do. One time I went to see her and she said something that sat me right down.

I'm a dead person today, she said. Would you fuck a dead person? Would you fuck me anyway even though I am a dead person? Or is there something else you want from a dead person—something special you want a dead woman to do?

I said what the hell are you talking about—and she started waving her hands real crazy and started explaining how she had some kind of syndrome that made her believe that she was dead. I said get out of here, there's nothing dead about you, besides how can you be dead and know that you have some kind of syndrome that makes you think you are dead—and so she promptly fell on the bed and played dead that whole night, and no matter what I said or what I did, she wouldn't stop pretending she was dead. So I did her while she laid there limp like that. She never moved, never made a sound—I mean I could tell she wasn't really dead, because I could feel her heart beating under me, but she wouldn't stop playing dead. I got fairly weirded out but I hung in there, pretending it was a game and I took my money's worth from her, even taking naps in between. Her body though—even playing dead and dead limp her body is something amazing. I felt weird doing it. It was so quiet in the room. And through the evening, I could swear that she was actually getting cooler. Like a dead person you know. Cooler and stiff and all that. But I kept doing her anyway, even when, towards morning, I could barely feel her heartbeat anymore.

I felt weird really weird. It even started smelling a little like a funeral home. But I knew that was just in my head, and it meant I had to get the hell out of there.

I bet the Mayor wants to appoint me to the Deshler school board. That's it, that has to be it. In this county, they don't elect people to the school board. All members are appointed by the Mayor himself. I know that the borough wants people that are upstanding citizens, clean cut and who will set a good example. Like me, I think I can do that. When I was in school, I was somebody that people looked up to. I even went to college where I aced all my classes, graduating Summa Cum, didn't even have to study that much. Things just came natural to me. They always have.

Christine says there aren't many men around anymore—she says that we are running out of men. Says that if I wasn't married and if she wasn't in the business and got a certain reputation that she needs to uphold, she'd go out and do the town with me. I laughed.

What kind of reputation do you have Christine?

Town whore of course, she said—a true friend to all men in need.

We laughed hard at that. We were sitting on the bed with nothing on and I had my arm around her and we were both sweaty from just having done it. I took out a copy of the book about the borough and I showed her my name in it. She was proud to see it, and she told me that she's proud to have me as a client and she knows that I am going places, and someday she wishes that she could come along.

I will be prouder than ever to fuck you then, she laughed. I will be better too.

Me, on the school board? Who knows what's after that. I could run for Mayor. People around town know my name. I'm almost a household word— everybody knows it. Bud's gas station has my name on it in big red letters. When you come in from Interstate 81, you see it there—my name—Certified Master Technician. Christine praises me every time she passes it—not like my Marcia. Marcia never talks about what a big man I am or how proud she is of me. That's because Marcia and I never should have got married—oh, I'll say it. I should have married Christine.

I feel bad for her though—living in that hellhole of a house with her hoarder mother. The place is truly disgusting, just like that Hoarders show on TV. Yes, this is up there with the worst of them. But, once you get through the mess, Christine's room is spotless, and you forget what kind of house is around you when you're with her. Everything around disappears when you're with her. Like—it's like she takes you someplace else. When I get to where I want to be in this town, I will do something to help Christine. Maybe I'll feed her some money to get her own place. Maybe I'll get to keep her to myself like a mistress. So she doesn't have to do all those other disgusting men besides me. And I'd get her some help too. Some help to get her straightened out. Maybe I'll even divorce Marcia and take up with Christine instead. But that would have to be after I get to where I want to be in this town. I've got this clean cut image to uphold—certified master technician and all. And besides, I still love Marcia. Her and the kids. I can't leave them, she's my wife. It would be wrong to do now, while the kids are little. Plus it wouldn't do anything for my image in the town. Got to keep it clean. Got to keep this business with Christine under wraps, or in my pants, so to speak.

I'm not afraid that Christine will spread it around town that I come to her—I've told her right out that that can't be, and she swore no one will even know—

Whore to client privilege, she said. I'm a professional, like a doctor. You know?

We laughed at that, and she said something about who would she tell about anything anyway? She says she's got no friends—well, she says she's got one. She says her friend lives in the house with her among the trash and filth and keeps hidden when people come over to visit her. I'm not sure how that can be, I've never noticed anyone besides her mother in the house, but I don't get into it with her. Not with my Christine.

See when we were going together back in high school, Marcia was entirely different than she is now. She was better at sex than Christine ever will be. Marcia was one hot potato. Not only was she the head of the cheerleading squad, but she could have had her pick of any of the guys that she wanted—football, basketball, baseball—but she chose me. She used to follow me around like a little puppy dog. Even then, she knew I was the big man. Everybody knew. We went together all through high school and then together through college and then just naturally, when we were just graduated and in our early twenties, we got married. We were hot together for a long time. But after she had the third kid, it seemed like she cooled off—a lot. I mean I still love her and I would never do anything to hurt her, but sex is pretty much over for us, maybe once or twice a year if I'm lucky. That's why when I found out about Christine, one of the guys at work told me about her, and when I went to her place—what a shock! The house was a wreck, like I said. When I opened the door, the stink hit me like a ton of bricks, and I barely staggered my way through the hallway and up the stairs, thinking the whole time—what have I gotten myself into. But then she turned out to be this wonderful woman, like I said. Sure, bizarre as hell, but worth every dollar. So I tell my wife that every Thursday I need to work the late shift at the garage; something about tank maintenance, and repair backlogs at the gas station. I keep the lights on and my car parked outside, just in case. And that's when I go to Christine's; every Thursday. And it makes me feel so much better about my wife—you'd think it would drive a wedge between us, but I think it has made our union stronger. With Christine's help I can look past the lack of sex between us, and the lack of passion in my wife, and see all her other great qualities—she's a great friend, a great cook, and a great mother. That's why I say, thank God for Christine—in a weird way, it seems bizarre to say this, but I believe that she has saved my marriage. I love Marcia and I love the kids and like I said— I would never do anything to hurt them—oh—and there's my house too; a very nice one—I certainly worked hard enough for it. I'm sure Marcia's waiting inside. It's ten on the dot—I'm right on time. The kids are in their beds. So here comes a little TV together with Marcia, a dry peck on the cheek and a little hug pat, and I'll be off to bed. I do love Marcia—and tomorrow is the Mayor. I know that the Mayor will have good news for me. I know this town and I know everybody in it who counts for anything, like the back of my hand, inside out. I'm in for the school board—and that will only be the start of good things to come.

∞ ∞ ∞

I went to see the Mayor. And it was about the Deshler school board all right. But it was shit. Pure shit. I'm all shook up about it now. My hands are numb—my hands always get numb when I'm shook up. The Mayor said it simple and fast.

As you probably already know, I'd like to appoint you to the school board, Barry, but there's a little problem.

What problem? I said.

The Mayor leaned forward in his chair and clasped his hands on his desk.

Barry, whenever we are considering someone for a position in this town, we do a thorough background check. Now you, of course, passed with flying colors. You're a pillar of the community as they say—everybody likes you, everybody respects you, everybody knows your name and thinks highly of you.

That's great, I said. But—what's the problem?

The problem is you've been seen going into Christine Zidar's house every week for some number of months now.

I played dumb, though ice filled my veins—but I controlled it.

Christine Zidar? Who is Christine Zidar? I said lightly.

She's a known prostitute. The only reason we haven't arrested her is because—well, there are reasons. We kind of look the other way from her—but when a person like you gets involved, well—this makes a problem. Do you go to Christine Zidar's house every Thursday? That's what my man said to me.

Your man? What do you mean your man?

The hair on the back of my neck stood up.

The Mayor raised a hand.

Barry, because you're a prime candidate for our school board, we've had someone watching you to make sure you're the man we think you are. This is how we do it in the real world, you know.

I sat up straight, my anger growing.

What do you mean— make sure I'm the man you think I am? This is—Mayor, with all due respect—this is the United States and it's wrong for the government to be spying on its people—

Not spying. Watching. And Barry, if we found out you have been with this woman on a regular basis, with just a casual check, the townspeople will probably know about this too. And if it gets around town that you've been seeing a prostitute, and that we've put you on the school board, well—a lot of people, including myself, could end up looking bad.

I thought of Marcia and the kids. I felt cold.

Who knows about this, I asked.

I do—and the private detective firm we hired to do the check— but they won't let it out. They're a reputable firm. They are professionals. Why, the records have probably been destroyed by now. That's what they do. They do a case, report on it, and then forget it. You don't have to worry about anybody else knowing.

So what about the school board?

He leaned back.

We got to first make sure that you stop seeing this woman. Then we've got to wait a while to make sure things are all cooled down.

Cooled down? I thought you said no one knows.

No one we know of knows. But Ms. Zidar lives in a residential neighborhood, and the neighbors have filed complaints both about her mother's hoarding and about the men that go in and out of there every night. Keeping this cool is getting harder and harder. The Zidars are probably going to be evicted soon, because the house is a health and safety hazard. They will be gone and forgotten.

Wow—I didn't know it was that bad—I mean I knew it was bad but—

Never mind, said the Mayor, sweeping his hand across his desk. I would not doubt you've been seen by the neighbors going in and out of there. So that's why after today, you have to stop going there. When that's been the case for a couple of months and they get evicted and the neighborhood cools down, we can reconsider you for the school board.

A couple of months?

I sat up straight.

That's right—and I wanted to tell you myself, man to man, about all this. To me and everybody else you are, as I said, a pillar of the community. We need to keep it that way. We can't appoint somebody only to have someone else step forward and say they've seen you go into that house. When we appoint you, the spotlight will be on you. I know what the spotlight is like. Trust me Barry, you have no idea what people are willing to do to take power away from people like us.

Thoughts of Christine went through my mind and I felt cold and my hands were numb and I mechanically said to the Mayor, Okay Gene—I appreciate the heads up. I won't lie. I have been seeing her. I've been doing it to save my marriage, if that makes any sense, but that stops now. You have my word on it.

Good, Barry, he said rising. He thrust out a hand.

I left the Mayor's office numb, just numb. And when I got to the car I saw Christine's face in the windshield and it hit me; after all my fantasies about taking care of her, just a single day later she was gone. Gone from my life.

I sat there for a while crying. Real tears—real tears. I hadn't cried real tears for as long as I could remember. I couldn't remember ever having done this. What will happen now, I cried. I miss her. I miss her. I started the car and drove out onto Main Street and wiped at my eyes as I drove. I felt hollow. I decided that I had to drive by her house, one last time. I don't know why this became so important but I had to do it. The gas station, the car repairs, Bud, they could all wait. I headed up toward her neighborhood and as I drove and the houses, poles, fences and hedges flowed by, I drove slower. I will never see Christine Zidar again. I repeated this in my mind. I thought of Marcia—poor, sexless Marcia and how I loved her. How I loved her so. As I drove I thought about how I could fix this hole in my marriage, in our lives, now that I don't have Christine by my side. I wondered how in the world will things work out?

When I came to her street, I turned down and there it appeared—the dark overgrown house with the yard of trash and the tattered shades between the two perfectly kept houses on either side with their manicured lawns—and I could see it, maybe for the first time, as I slowed past her house, what a terrible place they lived in and how terribly badly they had let it go. Disgusted, I sped up past it and the darkness of that house behind me faded and I left their street—and I thought how Christine was in that terrible house, my Christine trapped in there, under all that garbage. Other sick, disgusting men would continue to have her, and then I worried—but she'd be out three hundred bucks a week now. What would that do to my Christine? And then I thought there,

I have said it—My Christine.

My Christine!

Mine!

I pounded the wheel. I resented that other men would have her and would continue on having her and that she was gone to me and I resented her too, for not having chosen to be with me in high school and in college instead of Marcia and for not having given me the three perfect kids and for having such a magnetism—such a perfect body, custom built for fucking me, and such a beautiful face. My Christine.

I pulled up in the Shop-Rite parking lot away from all the other cars and I shut off the motor and I cried, My Christine! Oh my God I will never see her again. It hit me over and over again, and I smashed at the steering wheel at my life and what it had become and I cursed the damned Mayor and I denounced the school board as shit and all I wanted was to see my Christine, lying there, with that smile, having said something completely bizarre, like she would every time, but then motioning for me to come into her again. The gas station was not for today. I was feeling sick today—I would call Ross and tell him he would be running the place today, because I am sick. I drove out of the lot. I drove home. I went into the house and Marcia was there—I told her I was not feeling well—I told her and she said Oh Barry, you look awful, what's wrong—and she reached out and hugged me and I closed my eyes and Christine was there against me and I was embracing her for the last time and I drank her in and I opened my eyes and looked over Marcia's shoulder, at the blank kitchen wall, the tea towels hanging off the cabinets, and the coupon books on the kitchen tables and I squeezed her hard.

I love you, I said.

I love you too, Barry.

And at last I squeezed her harder for the last time.

I love you, I told Christine.

I love you always.

13 – The Process Server

A SMALL WHITE CAR WITH A THAYER COUNTY GOVERNMENT SEAL ON the door pulled up in front of Thelma and Christine's dark overgrown trashed house. From the small white car, a small man in a white shirt and black tie got out with a blue folder in his hand and he stood there a moment regarding the house. The house number was still visible so he came down the path through the garbage bags and up onto the littered sagging rotting porch and knocked on the dark front door. A long-dead Christmas wreath hung there. Needles fell as he knocked. Inside, Thelma stood in the kitchen listening to the knock and went to the stairs and called up for Christine. The knocking came again, louder this time and she called out softly again.

Christine! Christine, come down, I need you.

Christine!

Christine came down in a red robe and stopping halfway down the stairs she heard the knocking and told her mother, Mom—someone's knocking. Answer the door.

No! I need you to answer the door for me. I can't answer the door. Nobody knocks on my door at ten in the morning. I can't answer because I've never answered the door at ten in the morning before.

The knocking grew more insistent and Christine came down the rest of the stairs toward the door and as she passed her Mother she said, Well we've got to get it—what if it's important?

What could be so important?

We'll see—

Christine reached the door and opened it pulling the trash leaning against it over and it cracked open and a pasty white face appeared and she pulled it fully open and the man from Thayer county stood there in his dark short tie and short sleeved white shirt and he held out the blue folder.

Are you Thelma Zidar? he asked, obviously gazing past Christine into the terrible state of the room beyond.

No—no I'm not, said Christine, and she turned holding the door from slamming shut from the weight of the trash pressing against it.

Mom! she called. This is for you—there's a man here to see you.

Thelma stood cowering in the darkened kitchen, safe in the shadows and called back, I—I can't come to the door I'm not dressed—

Well you were dressed a minute ago—come on out and come to the door.

She turned back to the dark tied man.

I'm sorry about this, she said.

That's okay—what's your name. Do you live here?

Yes. I'm Chrstine Zidar. I'm Thelma's daughter. What is this all about?

Here, he said, holding out a blue folder. Here's a notice from the Thayer County Sheriff's office. A copy is also being mailed to you. I can leave this with you—what's your name?

He whipped out a small pad from his pocket and a pen.

Christine Zidar, she said—why?

I need to write down who I leave this with.

He wrote her name in the pad squeezing his tongue between his teeth and squinting into the pad. When he was finished, he said That's an eviction notice and notice of condemnation from the county—I was told your house was inspected a week ago. Is that right?

Christine couldn't hear him. The words Eviction Notice hung in her mind before the man and all the rest of the words had come out of him.

Eviction notice? she said—what? When—

She opened the folder. The effective date was a week away.

Yes. Your house failed inspection and is being condemned as a healthy and safety hazard. Here—step aside—I need to tack this note to the door.

He held out a yellow sheet and a thumb tack and Christine moved quickly and tore the yellow sheet from his hand, reading the single word on top.

CONDEMNED

No, she said, pushing it back in his face—you're not hanging that sign on my Mother's door.

Okay fine, then you do it, he said pushing back the note towards her and pushing the tack into the doorframe.

What is it? called out Thelma weakly, finally approaching from the shadows inside the house. Martin stood back, way back, deep in the dark.

What is that in your hand, Christine?

Mom—never mind, go back inside. I'll tell you later—

Good bye have a fine day, said the dark tied man, turning to go. And be out by that date. You've been served. Good day.

The man turned away and went down the lane between the garbage bags and went through where there used to be a gate and got in his car. The car started noisily. Christine let the door close and took Mother's hand.

Mom—this is a notice from the county. They want us out in a week.

Jesus Christ, said Thelma, her eyes rolling back in her head— Jesus Christ!

And she fell first to her knees and then flat out on the floor. The blood rushed down from Christine's face and she turned and threw open the door—the process server was still sitting in his car sorting his papers—she needed him since she didn't know where her mother's phone was under all the trash in the kitchen and so she called out and waved to the process server who luckily had his window rolled down.

Sir! she cried. Sir! Come help!

She looked down at her Mother who was white as a sheet and still as a corpse.

Come help! she screamed. Come help!

The man looked up and opened his car door. He came running up through the path as fast as he could.

What's wrong? he yelled as he came up the porch steps. What help do you need? Are you all right—

My Mother has collapsed—call 911—you have a phone?

The man got in the door and saw Thelma lying there and whipped out his cell phone and punched in the numbers for 911. As the phone rang he got on his knees next to Thelma and felt around her neck for a pulse. Yes, he said suddenly into the phone, in a voice oddly muffled as the surrounding trash absorbed the words—Yes, I need an ambulance right away at—

He tore the notice from Christine's hand and read the address into the phone.

—yes I need an ambulance. A woman has collapsed. She's out cold, she's not moving—yes I think there's a pulse—yes I'm here with her daughter. Send an ambulance quick—

Martin watched from back in the dark, unmoving, as the black tied man listened a moment and then handed the cell phone up to Christine.

They want to talk to you, he said, and as she took the phone he started mouth to mouth resuscitation on Thelma as he held her hand tight. Christine felt the phone numb in her hand and it went to her ear and she said Yes? Yes, I'm her daughter. Thelma Zidar. Yes that's her. I am Christine Zidar—him? He came from the county to see us this morning. He served us a notice and I showed it to her and she collapsed. An eviction notice. Yes she took one look at it and collapsed. Yes. Yes I will.

Sirens appeared in the air and grew louder and at last an ambulance pulled up behind the process server's car. As paramedics got quickly out Christine said into the cell phone Yes they're here— Yes. Okay I'm hanging up. Good bye.

She handed back the cell phone, but the process server was too busy still giving mouth to mouth to her mother to take it. Two beefy paramedics came up the walk laden with equipment. They wore blue and said to Christine as they approached the door Where is she? Where—

They paused a moment and looked around and into the open

door of the house and their mouths hung open as they took in the state of the property they were on. They pushed their way in past the door, and past Christine and told the process server We'll take over now bud—step back let us see her—

The one paramedic began working on Thelma as the other looked around the room, amazed.

You guys live here? he asked Christine and the process server.

No not me, said the black tied man. I work for the county—

I live here, said Christine. She's Thelma Zidar and I'm her daughter.

The enormity of what was happening struck Christine in the gut and forced the blood from her face—she steadied herself on the doorframe and the process server said You all right Ma'am? You look sick.

Wouldn't you be? she said strongly, waving the notice in his face. Beside this is all your fault! Look at my Mother. It's your fault, you and your God-damned notice!

I—I'm just doing my job. It's not my fault—

Yes it is! Look at my Mother!

Mother had an oxygen mask on and the Paramedics worked feverishly on her and a third Paramedic brought a gurney up the walk, with some difficulty, because the walk between the masses of trash in the yard was so narrow. God, muttered the Paramedic— God—what a shithole of a place! Do people live here? Do you people really live here?

Reaching Christine and the process server, the Paramedic said, Step aside please—step aside—

Where are you bringing her, said Christine. Which hospital?

Deshler General—step aside—Come on I have the gurney—

And at the instant her mother sat straight up and tore the oxygen mask from her face and pushed the Paramedics back away from her.

No! she cried.

There was dead silence as everyone froze and stared.

No one is taking me from this house! I'm not going to the hospital, I just fell down. I fall down—what's wrong with that? Don't you ever fall down? Do you kick a woman out of her house like you're doing just because she falls down? I'm seventy five I have a right to fall down!

Christine pressed a fist to her chest and said, Mom? Mom—you sound okay are you okay?

Thelma waved her arms waved for everyone to get back. The Paramedics rose.

Of course I'm okay, wouldn't you fall down too if you saw you were being thrown out of your house? Well it said that we have time, so you're not taking me anywhere today just because I fell down—we still have time—the piece of paper says that we still have time—so I'm staying right here—right in my home! If you take me now I know I'll never come back again!

Back in the unseen dark Martin smiled.

Thelma struggled to her feet and one of the Paramedics went to steady her by the arm but she pulled herself away, causing a bunch of trash to fall around them.

Don't touch me! she said stonily. Everybody, everybody—get out of my house! Leave me and Christine alone!

All right ma'am—but—are you sure you're all right—

Yes! Just a little tingly in the hands. Get out!

And Christine turned to the process server and said And tell your damned cronies down at the borough hall that there's no way we're leaving this house—you tell them that—

I can't tell them that, Ms. Zidar, there's an appeals process—you need to come down to the county and there are forms that you need to fill out and—

She waved her hand across his face, Shut Up, she said, never mind the process! Never mind the county! Never mind the forms! We're not leaving—now everyone get out!

Yes get out! Yelled Thelma struggling to the door and holding herself by the doorjamb.

Get out! she yelled once more.

Mother and daughter stood there sternly, arms crossed before them, Christine's red robe seeming ablaze and her Mother's black dress glowering down over the men.

The paramedics and process server retreated down the walk and the process server turned and called out Remember—a copy of the notice will come in the mail. It will outline the appeals process, like I said you can—

Fuck the process and fuck your appeals! yelled Christine.

Yeah! shouted Thelma, smiling at her daughter. She was proud of her daughter. They looked victorious and majestic in their door and they stood there a moment watching the men go and then they turned back into the house and slammed the door shut so hard that splinters of wood flew off the door frame. Inside Christine deflated. Together they went into the kitchen and Christine helped Thelma into her chair and then sat down herself.

Jesus Mom, she said. That was some way to start the day.

I'm not leaving my house, said Thelma shaking. They came to take me from my house but I'm not leaving my house—they meant to take me forever. Forever!

You don't have to go Mom, said Christine, touching her mother's shoulder. You don't have to. But are really you okay? You fell pretty hard there.

Martin stood impassive; always watching, always. Gone, but there watching.

Christine wiped a strand of hair from her mother's face as the woman answered.

I'm just a bit sore, I'm sure everything is going to be alright.

Christine hugged Thelma to her. She felt the old woman's frailty in her arms. With closed eyes she pressed the woman who had given her birth to her; and she thanked God that her mother was still alive and fairly healthy, she could not bear to be living alone without her. She reflected on how lucky she was to have someplace like this to live, with someone she loved so much and who loved her back. She overlooked the state the house was in and felt her mother pressing into her like a baby needing to be stroked and rocked and cooed to. With her eyes closed she imagined what it would be like to have a baby of her own. Someone to raise right, not like she was raised; someone to love and live with her until she, too, grew old. She held her baby like this for a long time and she imagined what kind of man her baby's father would be. Not foolish enough to die in a truck accident like her father had when she was just a baby. Not like any of the men who came to pay her for fucking. Her husband would be unlike those men—her husband would not have to go to a whore to get satisfaction. She would satisfy her husband better than any wife had satisfied a husband before. And as she held her baby to her breast she thought of the wives of those men who she serviced, and how ignorant they must be to not know what their husbands were up to. They would never be the kind of wife she could be. She would cultivate a sixth sense to know if her husband was satisfied. The same sixth sense she used now to be sure that she had fully satisfied her Johns. What would it be like to be married and to have no Johns and to have a baby and to live in a normal house, with clean bright rooms, and a welcoming front yard full of flowers, just like her neighbors; but then she thought of Thelma. Thelma would then be all alone in this house. If Christine had a normal life, and was a wife, with a happy husband and bustling child, her mother would be all alone then. And that would be horrible, for her to be fully alone. Her thoughts continued until the baby in her arms moved and pulled away and she opened her eyes and there was Thelma, looking up at her with eyes full of love like a baby would, an innocent little baby's eyes, that was what her mother's eyes were like. Like a baby's they looked at her with the wisdom that comes from innocence and unknowing, just being, just living. That was all her mother wanted to do. Live out her days in her house, with Christine.

Why can't we just be left alone? Christine wondered. Why do the neighbors have to be so terrible? Why can't they simply look the other way and let us live out our lives in peace? So what the house was a wreck of trash and clutter and darkness; they did not have to live here. They did not even have to look at our house when they come outside, there are many other nice houses in the neighborhood to look at, why do they have to focus all their attentions on ours. Busybodies, is what they are. They can't stand how we live. What business was it of theirs? What business? Christine eyed the crumpled up eviction notice lying near the front door. We had better not lose that piece of paper, she told Thelma. It is important.

She couldn't bear to look at the sign right now.

And imagine living in a house with a CONDEMNED sign tacked to the door like that man had wanted us to do? Condemned is a horrible word!

The most horrible word!

It was a word, though, that applied to them now, and this was horrible for Christine to think about so Christine stopped thinking it, rose and walked to the front door and picked up the crumpled eviction notice and placed it atop a pile of other garbage.

For safekeeping, she said to her mother. Just like everything else is in the house for safekeeping, right mother?

The jungle, always all around them, would protect them.

It is important to keep things in order, said her mother; it's like keeping pieces of yourself—and if anything is gone, we wouldn't be whole; and we would die. I would die living any other way, her mother said.

The moon; the sea; and the mountain would always protect them.

Christine knew this was true, and she wondered what would happen when—

Mom what are we going to have for breakfast, she said to her mother, to stop the thought from completing, because it was a horrible thought—just horrible.

I'm having some toast, answered her mother. I—I really shouldn't have anything at all, my stomach is in such knots, but one must eat, mustn't one?

Yes. One must eat, Christine agreed.

As twilight began to fall, the day passed. It passed by quietly; so quiet for such an important day, Christine marveled. They had their lunch together, and then they had their frozen dinners together, like they had every day. There were no Johns coming by tonight for Christine. There was nothing else to do today but for them to be together. Together they watched the tiny black and white television in the kitchen. They did not talk much; they never talked much. But together they laughed at the flickering images on the television until mother said that it was time for her to go to bed as twilight faded and after switching off the light downstairs, Christine followed her mother up to her own room.

She felt her way along the path through the garbage; and up the stairs. She got into her room, still wearing her red robe from when she had woken up. She had worn it for days now. She stripped it off and went into her bathroom and washed up. Christine came naked from the bathroom, and opened the window of her room, and there it was out there; the peak of Mount Everest with the bodies strewn all up and down around her. She closed her eyes and climbed out to sit on the peak and lift her face to the wind and open her eyes to the stars encompassing her, the moon shone down onto her brighter than she'd ever seen it before and though a mild wind blew, scattering snowflakes in the air, the night was warm. Out on the roof outside her window, naked at the peak of Mount Everest, she sat with the night expanded out all around her; infinite and eternal; the way she wished that her life was.

All the places she's been done and seen; jungle, sea, moon, and the mountain.

The beautiful icy mountain that would always be in her.

But life ends someday, always, she said to herself, and there are two ways down from the peak; the easy way, and the hard way. These bodies strewn around me have either gone down the hard way or started the easy way and ended up failing, she said sweeping her hands across the view in front of her. But she did not have to think about getting down, not tonight. In her mind she was peaking; she stayed up there all night counting stars and she only came in when the light began to come up and so she came down off the peak the easy way, back through the window, into her room. Once more she had avoided coming down from the peak the hard way. Once more she had avoided becoming one of the two hundred bodies strewn down around the peak. Once more, as she had done so often before, she slid the window closed, locked it, and she would sleep there until three in the afternoon the next day. Because that was when Whiteman comes over. That was always a funny day, she thought to herself as she fell asleep, wrapped in her red robe. It would be a funny day tomorrow. Whiteman is funny. He cheers me up.

14 - Mirrored-self misidentification

MACK WHITEMAN LAY BACK IN CHRISTINE'S BED PICKING HIS TEETH, using one of the supply of toothpicks he always carried in his shirt pocket for this purpose. The bedsheet was pulled halfway up his naked body and the many garishly crude prison tattoos on his body were visible. He shook his shock of grey hair and watched Christine, who sat in the vanity chair looking in the mirror. Suddenly, she turned.

Mack, she said pointing to her face. Who do I look like? Be honest.

You look like yourself, he said, waving the toothpick. Your big, beautiful self.

No I don't. I'm a brunette. When I look in the mirror, I'm some blonde with an ugly skinny face and no lips. I—watch. See.

She turned back to the mirror and saw a stranger looking back. The room seemed hazy.

Come here, she told Mack—come here and look in this mirror.

He rose and went to the mirror and looked in it with her.

Okay? he said—now what?

Who do you see?

I see you.

Well, she cried, tearing her hands down the sides of her head—

I see a stranger! A skinny, ugly stranger. Oh, no help from you—

And she shot up and grabbed at Mack Whiteman and pulled him to herself and buried her face in his shoulder.

Oh Christine, he said. That's nonsense. But here. Here—

He warmly embraced her and rocked her like a baby as they stood naked by the mirror.

Want to have another go, he whispered in her ear. I'm ready. Feel it?

No, she said, pushing him away. You need to tell me why I look that way in the mirror first. I must look the way I see myself in that mirror. Look at me Mack. What do I look like?

He recoiled at her urgency. Her grasping hands were up and her eyes were pies.

You look like yourself Christine, he said.

Yes and how is that? Describe me.

But you know what you look like—

I said describe me! she said strongly.

You have brown hair, brown eyes—high cheekbones, pretty lips, a cute nose—you're a pretty girl, he said.

She scowled.

You're lying. I'm a skinny blonde bitch with missing buck teeth.

God no! You have perfect teeth and you're not skinny or blonde—

Why are you lying to me Mack? she cried. Why won't you tell me the truth? What's wrong with you? Tell me what's wrong with you, that you can see that?

She sat back down on the vanity chair and held her face in her hands.

I—no—there's nothing wrong with me Christine—

He stepped up and put his hand on her shoulder. She shrugged herself violently away.

Yes there is, she said from her buried face. You're not seeing me right. Why won't you tell me the truth, of what you see?

She began to cry and Mack stepped back and looked at her.

What's the matter with you? he whispered. You are so smart, so alive, so good in bed—but so afraid of God knows what. I don't know how to help you Christine. I'm so sorry. But I just don't know.

Mack turned from her and returned to the bed and lay back down, pulled the sheet over himself, and spoke patting the mattress beside him.

Christine, he said—Christine come here. Let's do it again. I'm paying you for this time, you know that right?

She turned her head toward him while remaining hunched over the vanity top.

What do you see when you look in the mirror, she asked. Do you see yourself the way you think you look?

Of course I do. Come here, Christine.

Maybe you don't look the way you think you look. How do you think you look, Mack? Tell me and I'll tell you if that's what I see.

Mack rolled his eyes. Christine, this is stupid. Cut it out. Come here—

No tell me! she said, her eyes fierce.

Okay, he said, suddenly smiling. I'm a handsome blue-eyed grey-haired old man. Does that match what you see?

So far. What kind of lips do you have? What kind of nose?

I have—I guess I have thin lips and a fairly big nose. Come on Christine, this is stupid.

No! Not stupid! she said, and once more turned and buried her face in her hands. Mack lay there and started picking his teeth again. He was beginning to question if she was really worth it. Whenever he came to see her, she had another kind of problem that she put him through the wringer about. He wanted sex, not drama. He patted the bed beside him.

Christine, he said—I paid you three hundred dollars. Now, come here and earn that money. Forget all this mirror shit—you look like yourself, okay? You look good. Come on. My dick is hard as hell!

She spoke from her buried face.

No. I am too ugly. I need to quit this business I am too ugly to arouse any man.

You've got me aroused, he said. Look.

He pointed to the lump in the sheet where his erection stood waiting.

She glanced over, smiled suddenly, got up and came over. Okay, she said—since you paid I must be good enough for you. Here—

She lay down next to him and they had sex.

When it was over they lay together under the sheet and she looked at the ceiling and spoke idly in a flat monotone. He turned his head and watched her profile as she spoke.

Did you know that they're trying to put me and my mother out of the house? They served us with an eviction notice the other day. I threw it on the trash. They wanted to put a condemned sign on our door. I wouldn't let them. This is my room. This should always be my room. They can't just throw an old woman and her grown daughter on the street can they Mack?

She listened for his answer without looking down from the ceiling.

No, of course not, he said. He took her hand under the sheet and squeezed it. They've got to give you time. They've got to give you a chance to find another place.

But there's a date on it. It's next week.

The date means nothing. They just got to put some date down so they pull it out of the air. You just have to go down to the county and work it all out. You're going down to the county right Christine? To work it all out?

I—I don't know.

Fuck the process and the appeals, Christine had yelled the other day. Fuck the process and the appeals!

Well, you should. They'll give you time. They don't want people in the street or living out of their cars or anything like that.

Oh, I think they do, Mack. I don't think they give a shit about anybody. Oh, Mack—and she squeezed his hand—I don't know what we're going to do.

He raised himself on his elbow and looked at her.

Yes you do. You're going to go to the county and work it out.

She pulled her hand from his and looked away.

Everything is so crazy Mack. I'm seeing things, I'm hearing things—did I tell you that last night I was up half the night because the baby who lives under us wouldn't stop screaming?

What? What baby?

You heard me—there's a baby living somewhere under us, she said, bringing her hand up over her forehead and looking at the door.

Christine, listen. There's nobody living under you. This is not an apartment—

Leandra abruptly appeared in the door. She reached out her arms.

Leandra, breathed Christine, rolling away from Mack. Come to me my love!

What are you saying? said Mack, completely confused. Who are you talking to—are you talking to me? What? Christine, listen. Please pull yourself together—

Leandra came and sat on the bed smiling and took Christine's hand and she turned to Mack and said one word.

Hush.

What?

I said hush. I—I know we don't live in an apartment, like you said. Does that make you feel better? I know that. I imagine the baby. Okay? Does that make you feel better?

Leandra smiled over both of them and her smile warmed Christine as she continued to speak to the open-mouthed Mack.

I know what's happening with the mirror. That's not me I'm seeing in the mirror. That's somebody else.

But who were you talking to just then?

Christine and Leandra exchanged glances, and Christine looked at Mack and said Never mind that. I feel better now. I know I look like myself. That's just someone else in the mirror. Hey maybe I got here some kind of magic mirror—Mack go look in the vanity mirror and see who you see.

Christine this is crazy.

Go on. Do it.

He threw back the sheet and went naked to the vanity. As he went Leandra and Christine smiled together at how ridiculous he looked in those cheap black tattoos. He got to the mirror and looked in.

I see myself Christine. I see myself so I must not have the same problem you do.

I have no problem, said Christine. What problem?

I—uh, no. No problem. Christine, I think I am going to go now. I think you earned your money tonight.

Leandra frowned at Christine and Christine frowned at Mack.

What? No. It's only nine o'clock. You get another hour. I don't want to be—

She paused. He looked at her as he pulled on his underpants.

What? he said—what don't you want?

I don't want to be alone. Please stay—tell you what. I'll give you the whole rest of the night free.

You got me spooked Christine, he said, as he pulled on his trousers. You talk about the mirror, you talk to yourself, you tell me that you hear babies crying at night all night—Christine, I'm going to leave. Just try to get some sleep. I think that should help.

Leandra and Christine frowned at one another and Christine thought Well if he's leaving anyway and he thinks I'm crazy why not let him think I'm really crazy he—

We could make it a threesome, she said. If you stay. We can make it a threesome. For free.

He paused buttoning his shirt.

What? he said. You'd get another girl to come in?

Leandra laughed sitting on the edge of the bed, but said nothing.

Why—yes! That's what I'll do. I'll get another girl to come in. Will you stay?

What will I have to pay—?

I said it's for free.

Okay, he said. Do it.

Do what?

Leandra looked on smiling.

Call the other girl. Is she clean?

Oh yes. Very clean.

She squeezed Leandra's hand under the sheet.

Okay, he said. Let's do it.

She glanced at Leandra and Leandra let go her hand and got up and went over and began caressing the half naked Mack all over—caressing, and kissing, and pressing hard against him.

Okay there you go, said Christine.

Leandra kept pushing on top of him, harder.

What do you mean, there you go, said Mack. Who's here? I don't see anyone here.

Leandra was all over him; Christine smiled and lifted her arms and said I'm here—come to me, while we wait for her.

But you haven't made any calls—

Oh no—I arranged for this as a surprise for you. Isn't it your birthday soon? Isn't it?

No—

Leandra tongued Mack in the ear.

Well I thought it was—you've been such a good customer I thought I'd give you a surprise—she'll be here any time now. That's why you shouldn't leave—but let's not waste my time or your money—come here—take off those pants and all that other stuff that you've got on underneath and come here to me!

Leandra tore at his shirt and ripped open his pants following the movements of his hands and she was all over him still, as he said, All right and got the clothes off and moved toward Christine. Leandra clung to him but he moved so easily that you'd never know she was hanging onto him with her hands all over him; hands and tongue. Christine tried hard to keep a straight face as the two of them came into the bed with her. She rolled over and embraced Mack and went to work. The two women, one visible, one invisible, worked Mack over for a while and he writhed on the bed and Christine finally whispered in his ear.

How do you like us Mack, huh? How do you like us?

What? he moaned. Who's us—?

Us. Me. I am two women. I am three women. I am fifty, a hundred women all over you.

Maybe a million women Mack. Maybe all the women in the world or the universe!

Leandra and Christine laughed and Mack lay under them as they worked and he forced out the words Where's the other girl? What universe? Where—

Here! We are all here! Just for you.

And he shuddered and moaned and closed his eyes and Christine got off him and Leandra set on the edge of the bed smiling at Christine and Mack lay there a while breathing heavily until his eyes opened and he said Where's the other girl? I don't see any other girl but God—

God what? said Christine.

God, you're good. You talk crazy but you're good. You're as good as a dozen girls.

Leandra and Christine giggled at each other and at him.

Funny? he said. What is funny?

Oh nothing.

Where's the other girl you were going to bring here? When will she get here? I can't imagine what it will be like with—two of you.

Leandra and Christine giggled together again.

What am I that funny? said Mack, slightly annoyed. Why don't you answer me? Why are you acting so weird?

I'm not acting weird, she said. You're acting weird.

What?

What I said. You have had us, Mack.

She and Leandra stared at him.

What?

I said you have had us. We're done. You can go now.

Leandra melted back away through the door and was gone.

Now there's just the two of us Mack. And I'm done for the night. So get out.

What about the other—

Get out! I have gone off duty! Get out!

Christine got up and went to the mirror and sat and looked at the stranger who looked back at her, dead in the eye and she said I am not afraid of you anymore. I'm not afraid of you or anyone else that pretends to be me. You are not me. You are a stranger. I—

As she went on talking into the mirror this way, Mack Whiteman quietly got up, quickly got dressed and left a fifty dollar tip on the bed for Christine and left without saying a word, but all the while staring at her babbling into the mirror—and when the door closed behind him, she brought her hands to her face and squinted her eyes and laughed at how foolish it all had been to play with Whiteman; so foolish, but fun.

A good night's work deserved a good night's sleep, she said to herself. She went in to her bathroom, washed up, came out and shut the lights off and got under the sheets and Leandra returned to her and together they lay there silently quietly for the rest of the night until Christine rose the next day at ten with a tremendous smile on her face and she went to the mirror and she at last saw herself there as it should be—as it was all before. What a relief! she thought to herself. What a relief!

15 – Mount Everest V

EVEN MY FATHER USED TO SAY IT; MACK WHITEMAN, YOU'RE A CRAZY little son of a bitch. And to my brother Tom, too, he used to say the same thing—leaving me to wonder what my mother thought about being called a bitch. But I guess I feel I've always been a little crazy; a little wild, in a weird kind of way. That's probably why I never married; too busy running around, fooling around, messing around. You know like that. But I got serious. I run my father's cabinetry business. I'm busy from six to nine every day, including Sunday. But I sneak away from the shop on Tuesday nights. That's when I see Christine—see, I don't have time for dating or to go places and to do things where I might meet a regular woman. So instead I got this regular thing with Christine Zidar. My brother, Tom, told me about her.

My man, she is the best whore in all of Thayer County, and that's a fact.

And he was right. She is. But she certainly is weird and crazy wouldn't you know it? For that, she got me beat. She's not little on any of the crazy things. She told me one time, when she was laying there, that she was in a boat—come in with me, I'm in a boat—let's play that. Who could think of that? And tonight—the baby and the threesome thing—I don't know how she does it but sometimes you'd swear she had four hands. Like I said she's the best—best I've ever had. But at the same time she's truly creepy. Like when she gets that look in the eye—I really don't know what to think then. Where she is? Where has she gone in her mind?

Sometimes I am scared to be with her. But now, here, away, I am safe.

Anyway. I run the custom cabinetry business here in Deshler. My Father had it for years since before I was born. And it killed him. We used to have a big factory where we made all kinds of great high-end cabinetry for people all across the country. We didn't always only sell cabinets and shelving we got from other suppliers and manufacturers. My Dad built this big factory here in Deshler up from practically nothing. And it burnt to the ground one night when I was twenty, imagine that— a big, raging fire. We had a lot of solvents glues and shellacs and stuff like that in there, all in bulk. There was also a lot of nice wood, and barrels full of shavings too. This fire was a big fire, it was at night—and it was hot—hot as hell—even a block away you could feel the heat. You couldn't get close. It was in the summer. All the stars were out and the smoke went up and spread out and blotted out a huge swath of stars. We made the papers with this one. Pictures and all. But that was the end of my Father. He was already old by then, but the fires killed him. After that he sat in his chair in our house, he wouldn't eat, he wouldn't talk. He died in that chair with the television on. Mom came down in the morning and there he was, dead. After the fire I handled all the paperwork for insurance and all that. I set up everything to get the business going again. We opened a small store in the middle of Deshler. We started making cheap cabinets in the back.   The store didn't burn down. Mom told me, run the place—I can't do it. I don't know how to run a business, I had never even driven a car, and I never got past eighth grade. But this is what she said so I ran the business alongside my brother Tom. I handled all the books and paperwork while Tom was out front, selling everything that we had. It was a nine to nine business, seven days a week. My Father taught me all about that—he said having Saturdays and Sundays off was invented by the Church to slow us down and keep us under their thumbs. I can't remember the last day I had off. I think we closed the store when my Father died for three days. The destruction of the factory had put the business in a tailspin. But I pulled it out, with my brain—as my Father used to say—he'd point to my head and poke it.

Feels hard as a damned rock but there's a red hot brain in there son!

Anybody can get anywhere with a red hot brain!

Don't ever be afraid to use it!

Hot Mack! I call you hot Mack with the red hot brain!

And I did what he said. I've used it. I've used it all my life. But like I said, it's a little crazy too, just like Christine. It must be to push me like it does. Some days, I want to pull it out of my head and wring it out like a sponge and get the hot water out of it and slow it down a bit.

Since I was a child, the only time I was away from the family business was when my Dad sent me to West Point. I don't know how he did it, but my Father had connections, from selling fancy cabinets to people in high places. But it was mostly a waste, since I can barely remember my time at West Point. The haze of booze and drugs and all that is laid over my memories from there like a film. I remember I went to a wedding in those days—a friend's wedding, but I got so high out in the car on pot and pills that when I came in I just sat at the table at the reception wanting to throw up and my brain went in and out and in and out of being there, and I was—you know—I was white as a sheet, I felt like throwing up and so I held onto the table edge to keep myself from falling down in my fancy West Point uniform that I was wearing. I also didn't want to throw up on my uniform. I had to buy my uniforms, they didn't just give them to me, I had to buy them, and they weren't cheap. They had some reasoning about us being gentlemen with money, not accepting something for nothing, and so we had to buy everything. Well since I would have ruined my dress uniform if I had thrown up at the wedding so I just kept gulping the puke back down, swallowing every mouthful. And I made it through the ceremony. That's all that I remember from my time at West Point.

That day will be surrounded by a fuzzy haze for the rest of my life.

It wasn't long after that wedding I got thrown out of West Point and I went to prison. I was in prison for five years for selling pills that I got from a buddy who was a pharmacist, to the other cadets. It was in prison where I got my tattoos. It might be funny but I always wondered why my going up the river didn't bother my Dad. At least not that I saw. But he always was a hard man, so I guess he just understood that I had to make my own fuck ups. Hard that is, until that fire twenty years later that sent him into his chair and finally killed him. It also ended up killing Mom because she couldn't stand to be alone without him. She lasted six months after Dad died. Everyone says that she died of a broken heart. She just coasted her life to an end, just like when you are in a car and you shut it off and throw it in neutral and it just slowly, slowly, coasts to a stop. The engine ain't running any more. Her engine shut off when they closed Dad's coffin. You could see it in her face. She was switched off from that point on.

But about these tattoos; I got them in the jailhouse. I was crazy but like Dad said I had a brain; I just got the tattoos on my body. Not on my arms, hands or face where they would show and give people the wrong impression after I got out. I knew I was getting out in five years. And I knew that when I did I would be a big shot.

See this tattoo here? This is supposed to be a turtle. It doesn't look like a turtle, but it is one. I got it to remind myself to slow down—I felt that in those days I was on some kind of natural speed, I was always going at least a hundred miles an hour so I got the turtle to slow me down. And see this? This is a crab. A crab as in crabby. I was always crabby, my Mom would say—crabby baby, crabby boy, stop being so crabbing. So I got the crab tattoo for my Mom, though I never dared show Mom or Dad the tattoos after I got out of prison. See this one? A skeleton with a gun pressed to his head? About to be shot? Doesn't the gun look real? It's for my Dad. Many times he pressed his finger to my head and tell me that there's a hot brain in there—while he did that, he'd make his hand in the form of a gun and press the barrel finger to my head and pretend to shoot—and after he shot he'd say, well not anymore, now it's a cold brain like the rest of us got—and he would laugh and laugh all raspy and choking. I always hated it when he did that. My mother told me that the fumes in the cabinet factory made him a little bit crazy and that we need to cut him some slack. She also said that he was always crazy like me. So this skeleton tattoo is for him, and all these other ones. Here's a drum set, for my brother. He had a drum set when we were kids and it was in the cellar and he used to bash away at it in the middle of the night. Then one night at the climax of the song that he was drumming along to, because of the wine that he was drinking, he put his drumsticks right through the heads of his floor tom and snare drum and after that he never touched the drums again. It was like someone reached inside him and turned off the drum switch. He just lost interest. But he was never any good anyway. He tried to practice, but all the while he was just messing around. This tattoo is for him. And for Mom? Here—this big sunburst—in the middle—it symbolizes when I came bursting out of her.

You just bursted out of your Mother that day, Dad would say when he'd had a few joints.

You just went and bursted clean out of her gut.

I put it in her, and then it grew, and bursted right out! And there were you!

So that's where I got the idea. The sunburst is Mom and me at the moment of my birth. An important day, that. Without that day, I wouldn't be sitting here right now. And my Dad's cabinet store would have folded by now, or shut down after the fire. My brother is no good at the business side of it. Without me, he'd be a shoe shine boy down at the train station now, instead of decked out in some snazzy suit standing out front schmoozing customers to buy this table or these chairs or that cabinet. That doesn't take a brain. That's just the outside part of him going through the motions while the brain part of him is asleep. My brother's brain parts have always been asleep. Just awake enough to keep him breathing and thinking that he's got to walk around, got to keep moving—got to digest his food. And all those kinds of automatic things. But there's no thinking in my brother. That part of him is turned off. Poor Brother—he's so damned dumb. But enough about the fucking tattoos. The rest speak for themselves. But those are the important ones.

Prison was a trip though, wow! Such a fucking trip.

In prison—guys were getting their faces, arms, hands tattooed. I wasn't that stupid. Getting a tattoo is really a dumb thing. But I'm a dumb guy in many ways. About equal in intelligence to the dog I used to have when my brother was playing with his drums. About equal in intelligence to my bitch Sally. Sally. What a dumb name for a dog. My parents named her, and I never asked them Why Sally? I wish they were still alive for that one reason only—so that I could ask them why they named that dumb dog Sally. But, dumb as she was, Sally was a good girl. I wonder who the real Sally was—I mean who the dog was named after. I imagine that this was what they were going to name my sister who was stillborn. So they got a dog instead and gave the dog the name so their real Sally wouldn't be forgotten. But if they did that it was a mistake because dogs only live a fraction of what a person lives. Sally, oh Sally— I often wonder where she is now, dumb dog. In a pet cemetery someplace—that's something my mother would have done, that. She would've paid for a plot at a pet cemetery, and Dad would've gone along with her, because they had plenty of money most of their life. They'd buy whatever they wanted, whenever they wanted it. We had a big house, a great big split level that they got cheap because it was directly under some high tension electrical wires. Even though they had plenty of money but they always went for the cheapest deal just because that's the way my mother was. Now Dad, he was the opposite. He'd piss the money down the drain just because he could, he never haggled or negotiated—like with cars. People like to talk about making deals on cars. Has anybody ever really got a car dealer down in price? No. The dealers price the cars too high so they can seem to have come down and given you a break but the final price was what they really wanted all along. People are just stupid. You can't beat the system. Like for example, take Christine. She charges a hundred an hour and I pay her three hundred for three hours every Tuesday. Now I know all she really wants is fifty an hour. How do I know this? Trust me. She's a businesswoman. I could argue her down to where I would pay her just a hundred and fifty for my three hours. But I choose not to. Judging by the state of her house, she needs all the money she can get. So I pay the three hundred and throw in a fifty dollar tip, even though I know I could get her for less. But even at the lesser price, I think I'm going to have to stop seeing Christine pretty soon because she's really getting more and more bizarre each time I see her. Bizarre people like that end up doing bizarre things—like all of a sudden pulling out a gun from some place and going Okay, the person in the mirror has just told me to kill you, and I'd end up taking a bullet or two for her craziness. Now, don't get me wrong, I don't think Christine would actually do this—but I sense that sometimes she's hearing voices or seeing things that aren't there. So she may end up taking the advice of one of her voices. She may end up plugging a bullet or two into me if her voices tell her to. Or worse, like taking a knife to me. There've been women that have cut off their man's private parts—I don't know what I'd do if she were to do that to me. Anyway, back to the reason that I probably should stop seeing her anymore—tonight at Christine's, on the way out, I saw a great big mess of black bugs swarming around a raw pork chop lying on the floor, just outside the kitchen. Now what was a pork chop lying on the floor for? I know Christine's mother is the problem. She's a fanatical hoarder. Just look at the place. God knows what is under all those piles of junk. What kind of whatnot could be living under there, feeding, breathing, and waiting? But waiting for what? For the place to be cleaned up? Fat chance. Hah. Fat chance. I like that. But under those piles the wood floors and walls are rotting and what Christine and her mother don't know is that a hoarder's house just deteriorates when left to rot. The wood rots, the pipes leak, the shit flies—no, I was kidding about that. But the houses do begin to sway and lean and end up crashing down to the ground. I remember a little blue house off a few miles outside of Alexandria—it had cockroaches, and there were so many of these cockroaches that the neighbors started having problems too. So they condemned the place and ended up having to bulldoze it to the ground because the whole foundation was rotten with breeding cockroaches. Now I don't know if that little blue house was as packed with shit as Christine's house but it probably was to be breeding all those bugs. I myself couldn't live in a house like that. I couldn't sleep at night in a place like that. I've got good ears—I'd hear them munching all through the night. I wonder if Christine hears them munching too. Her room is clean enough. I've never seen a bug in her room and it smells nice too. She must spray it with some stuff. It smells like a woman's room—airy and sweet—tottering on top of that wreck of a rotting house. Except for the tiny attic, her room is at the very top of the house, like a nice clean golden crown on top of a filthy stinking, dying, rotting fat old pervert of a king.

She tells me that sometimes she goes out on the roof. She tells me some shit about it's Mount Everest out there. About how people died there and just stay where they fell forever. It fascinates her. Why do people want to climb the damn thing if all they are going to be doing is stepping over the dead people that fell before them? The place is very creepy, she says—like a big ice cream sundae with dead ants sprinkled all on top! I've asked her what was wrong with her mother and why the house is all hoarded up like that, and she got all pissed off at me. Lord God, she did!

There's nothing wrong with my fucking Mother. How dare you say that!

And there's nothing wrong with this house. This is how we like it!

We like it the way it is, how it was meant to be!

Okay, I said—I'm sorry I said that—and she went on to say that the house was taking advantage of her mother, taking over like it did, and cluttering itself all up like it was. She said while she was in the hospital her mother had to work hard to keep the house from overwhelming her room and she spent all her time in the room keeping the rest of the house out. She says that the shitty garbage just grew from nothing in the house; like an evil. The shitty garbage started to grow after Christine's Father died. Christine says her mother believes that the garbage is all one thing taken together, and that thing is the ghost of her dead husband. She says the house is really haunted. This is what Christine says of her Mother. But I don't know. She says these things when she goes into that spooky trance she does when she sits in front of that mirror on the vanity. After we have sex, usually. And that gets pretty weird, too. I could list all the services that Christine provides when I say have sex, but it's not hard to imagine what they are, I don't have to tell anyone. But I don't judge her, she's got her business and I got mine. We're both business people. I tell the guys down at the shop that I need to go to a business meeting every Tuesday— a meeting of local business men, this is what I tell them. Lord do I get horny after I walk out of the store and get in my car and head towards her place. I start thinking about Christine and her smell; the room's smell. And her mind. Well, maybe that's gone or going or what. But I don't go there for her mind. I just go there for my weekly fix. I've got the addiction every guy has. Isn't that something? I'm just like every guy. Even my brother Tom who is married—he's found time for all of that as well. But I couldn't—I could never get married myself, but I still got my itch to scratch—that itch that all men have—that curse. The need to blow the nose, as the philosopher put it. That weird old philosopher I read about in prison. They do a lot of weird things there in prison. And so do I, so who's to judge me?

16 – In the Half Moon Motel

THE SUN SHONE DOWN ON LEANDRA AND CHRISTINE AS THEY WALKED on the grassy lot where Thelma's house used to be. The houses on the street were a row of teeth with a gap where one had been pulled. Condemned houses, rotten beyond repair get torn down, said Leandra—and infamous houses like those where killers lived or crimes were done like mass murders get torn down, and all that remains is a grassy space. The city takes over and the grassy space remains and it briefly becomes a memorial to what happened there, what lives were lost, and what lives were changed. I could name a whole handful of killers and crimes where this has happened, like the Berdella house in Kansas City, Missouri. Six men were tortured to death there. Imagine?

But they'll rebuild a house here right? said Christine—being the house of a hoarder doesn't make it an infamous house.

They joined hands as they stood regarding the fresh new grass. A clean breeze washed over them. Leandra looked around and at Christine and told her Well, there is one case of hoarding where the house was torn down and a green space remains. It's the house of the Collyer brothers in New York City.

Collyer brothers? What makes the Collyer brothers so special? Never heard of them.

Oh, yeah; they were famous hoarders in the forties who packed their house with everything including an entire automobile. They died in the house and nobody knew, until the neighbors complained about the smell and the city went in—it made a sensation. It took weeks of digging through over 140 tons of trash to find the bodies. They had little rooms in the garbage and tunnels through it and stuff and they died because it all collapsed on them one day.

How do you know all this, Leandra? said Christine, as she lifted her face to the sun and the warmth spread across her face down her neck to her arms, raising goosebumps.

Like I told you, when you were in the hospital, I read what I could. And because of that, I know things. As a matter of fact I know that hoarding is sometimes called Collyer Brothers' Syndrome because of these brothers.

Christine continued to hold her face up and the sun poured onto her and came down in her body and worked with the mild breeze washing over her to cause her to open her eyes, and there she was, sitting on the edge of her bed back inside the house looking at the cold hard wall. Leandra was gone, the grassy space was gone, and the house was still here, gently breathing around her. Christine wondered what the date was on the eviction notice that lay crumpled up in a ball atop the mounds of garbage in the kitchen. Neither she nor her mother wanted to know about that notice, Thelma especially wanted to make it so they never got it, and so did Christine, though she did think about it once in a while and wondered what was going to happen when the date finally came.

Who will come? What will they do?

She squeezed the bedspread tightly to herself as she went on thinking They may come with sirens blazing and force us out of the house and then where will we live, where will we go?

She glanced at the window a moment and a voice came behind her and said the car—you'll have to live in the car. Mother's Lincoln is big enough. You can live in the car.

She turned around and behind her was the showroom of the Lincoln dealership and there sat their car gleaming, brand new and glowing, huge and wide and tall in the bright lit showroom with the red and yellow and green bright painted walls and the shiny-faced fat salesman in a gleaming white shirt came from behind the car and came up to her and Thelma.

Interested in the big Continental four door? he oozed, rubbing his hands together. I can see you got that look. I know the look. I've seen it a million times.

Yah I think we're interested, said the women in near-unison.

We need to live in it. How many bedrooms does it have?

The car stood there waiting, huge.

Oh, said the salesman—sure, it has four bedrooms. It has four bedrooms, a kitchen, a living room, a family room and two full baths. Can I take you through it? I'd love to take you through it. It'd be lovely to live in—just lovely. Come on in, don't be shy—

He stepped loosely over towards them, swung the big door open and motioned them forward. Thelma and Christine climbed into the car followed by the salesman. He swung the door back closed with a sound like a bank vault swinging shut. Past the big leather-covered steering wheel stretched the long wide leather seats and a new car smell that overwhelmed them. They stepped past the seats into the kitchen and the salesman's booming voice echoed off the broad clear windshield. Thelma stepped forward and ran her hand along the dashboard counter top. Christine tried the sink; the water flowed. Beyond, the refrigerator, dishwasher and oven set into the far door glowed of the fresh new stainless steel all around them.

Behold your kitchen! said the salesman.

Wow, said Thelma. And look Christine, look! This is just exactly like my kitchen at the house used to be years ago—when Martin was still alive.

Yes, there's no trash—

The passenger side window above the sink was trimmed by a beautiful curtain which was pulled back and rolling hills and fields stretched off into the distance under the yellow sunlight.

Perfect, thought Christine, for long evening walks with Leandra.

So step through this door! said the salesman, fingering his tie, smelling a sale—back here is the dining room! Come on around the seatback there—look!

They walked around and Christine was amazed that they didn't even have to stoop. They came around the passenger seat past the door and there was a large dining room with a fine brown stained walnut dining room set, and a wonderful crystal chandelier. They went into the dining room.

My word, breathed Thelma.

The room was clear of trash from door to door and it was exactly like her own dining room, as it had been before. She stepped in and steadied herself on a chairback. The new car smell mixed with the smell of new wood and new leather and new shellac.

This is great Mom, said Christine—and look.

Out the window spread rolling pastures dotted with black and white happy dairy cows all feeding on the lush happy grass and Christine just had to ask.

Where's the showroom, she said to the salesman. Out the windows are fields and pastures—where's the showroom?

You're experiencing the car now ma'am, said the salesman. Everything you see is part of the experience of this fine, fine American-made luxury car.

He grinned a moment as the women drank this in, then he said, and over here—through these doors—

He slid back a beautifully done pocket door and the living room was there, complete with nice big couches and two matching green La-Z-Boys and with a large flat screen TV against the back of the front seat. They stepped into the room. The rear seats of the car stretched across to the other side where a beautiful lace curtain adorned the driver's side rear window.

And through there are the bedrooms, and the baths, said the salesman, pointing to a seatback that pulled down to reveal a door and everything was gleaming shiny clean and free of trash. There was Christine's bedroom—with the vanity dresser and her bed, and the window, outside of which—she pulled back the curtain and shade a bit—outside of which was the peak of Mount Everest, tall and windblown with a plume of snow off it looking like the picture in the National Geographic magazine at the hospital that got her all onto this. She let go the curtain. They went on to see Thelma's room, and her private bath, and came out the back door and into the showroom. The salesman closed the back door and the three of then stood in the shining light next to the big Lincoln.

There, the salesman said—you could live fine in that—and I can give you a great deal. I can put you in this car for—well, wait. Let's go over to my desk. I need to look at the data sheet on the car to give you an exact price. But it'll be more than reasonable for what you'll be getting. Come on.

He led them toward a row of desks and chairs against the back wall but Thelma looked to the right and was stopped dead in her tracks. A truck stood there, and a man. A red pickup truck, gleaming and new and the man standing next to it was her husband Martin, back just like he was before. She rushed up to him.

Martin!

The red truck stood beside a lovely house with the big SOLD sign on the front door and it was before Christine and before all the hoarding and before Martin's accident—and they embraced.

The salesman and Christine stood back watching with great grins on their faces as the two spoke beside the house in the stone driveway and the truck, gleaming new and undamaged.

Martin! Thelma pleaded. Now that you're back we're going to make sure you get enough sleep so that you don't fall asleep at the wheel like you did before. You won't ever crash again like you did. Promise me.

No, I promise, said Martin. He pulled off his glasses—I'm here to buy this truck. I need a truck for all my upcoming contracting work—are you going to buy that car? I saw you come out of it— that's a great car, you've got a great eye.

They both glanced toward the Lincoln and the big front porch stretched across it brand new and spotless, free of trash, swept clean and new, and Thelma looked back to Martin and said, Well now that we're married you need to make a living, and we need a place to live together in, and I think this red truck and that Lincoln car are the answer.

He nodded. Christine stood mute, a shade of their wonderful

future before them. The salesman grinned and said Well I'll be at my desk—come over when you're both ready. And he walked away whistling, a car and a truck sold in just a couple of hours, yessiree!

Christine opened her eyes a little sitting on the edge of the bed—in the mirror she saw her Mother and Father standing over her and she thought, So this is what it was like before I was born. I was a little imp—a little ghost of a kind—and she closed her eyes and let Thelma and Martin go on talking, Thelma rubbing Martin's arm.

Red, she said, regarding the truck—I've always liked red, it really is a great color.

Fire engine red, grinned Martin—the best. What color will you take the Lincoln in?

We're going to take the floor model—we just went through right there.

The silver Lincoln Continental stretched across from wall to wall and it shone—perfectly, there were no dings, no jagged gash along the side. No years yet. No years.

Perfect, said Thelma. We can live in there. We're being put out of the old house you know.

I know, said Martin. But this is better. The Lincoln is brand new. You won't let it get like the old house now will you?

No not as long as you are here.

She looked at him lovingly.

Come on, she said, taking him by the hand. Let me show you the bedroom—of our new house.

He smiled. They went across and she opened the back door of the Lincoln and they got in and shut the door. Christine looked toward the salesman. He tapped a pencil against his desk. He put his finger to his lips, and he winked. Christine smiled, nodding. The moment of your conception is what you're not supposed to witness, he said. And she didn't witness it—it was in the bedroom in the back of their new Lincoln. She smiled knowing that she was being brought into the world—at the thought that even though they didn't know her yet, that they wanted her. She turned from the Lincoln and from Daddy's new truck and went across to where the salesman sat, with a pencil tapping on the desk, wearing a great big grin.

Sit down young lady, he said. Sit down and stretch yourself. There's no rush. They can take their time. It takes time to make something as great as you.

Oh please, you flatter me, she said sitting.

He leaned back twirling the pencil.

So—you say you're going to be living in the car as well. Why is that, if I may ask, that is?

We're being put out of our house. Mom's a hoarder.

Oh really? And people complained?

Yes. The town condemned the house and we have to get out.

When?

The date is on the balled-up eviction notice my Mom threw into the trash. We don't know the date. I guess we'll know when the County comes calling.

So—this is kind of like the way life is.

What? How?

Because, he said, leaning forward. You live your life not knowing when the end is coming, and you're rolling along on your merry way and then one day poof! Sure, maybe the date's written on some piece of paper somewhere, but you ball it up and forget about it, never having read the date, and then suddenly you're gone. Just like that eh? The end comes when you least expect it. Isn't it like that?

He nodded as she answered.

Yes I suppose it is like that.

Well then you're lucky I'm here. Since you need a car, you know.

Oh—Mom already has a car—one just like that one—but old and all beat up.

We'll we could take it for a trade in. But, you know, actually we already have it. That Lincoln Continental you went through? That one right there? That's your mother's car, brand new again. Couldn't you tell?.

She looked out at the car. The tall three story car with the wraparound porch that looked like new and set in the middle of the row of teeth run up and down the block.

She turned back to the salesman and said This is—this is all too much. I'm getting dizzy—

No you're not, the room around you is.

The room is dizzy? Around you and I here? Here—?

And Christine opened her eyes in her bedroom and the room was shrunk down around her like she was shrink wrapped in the room and it was all black—and a light appeared. A light that appeared to be coming closer and the shrink wrapped room released her and she was born, and the light came around her and she was in her Mother's arms and she rose, where she went to the dresser and put her hand on it. And there she swore like on some big bible. She swore that she'd love Thelma forever, lying there in her arms. And after she swore that she'd love Thelma forever, her room was around her again, and she sat on the bed again unsure of where she'd been—it was all hazy still and grainy too when she tried to look back at it all. But now she was here and the future was before her and she thought about the next step of her problem—of what to do when the day came when they were going to be evicted. Where would she bring her Johns? The big car was too new, too clean, too pure to be sullied by her clients and their moaning and groaning and their cigarette smoke and their dripping slime and their stinking stubs in the ashtray. Her room atop the house now would be in the car if she wanted it, sure, but she thought of the Half Moon motel down on highway thirty six. She had taken a John there once when she was just starting out and the room was perfect. She had sat in the Half Moon motel, looking around. The bed had a pleasant red checkered spread like a tablecloth, the light was bright and cheery, the side chairs were plush and new looking, and there was nothing dated about the place though she knew it had probably been there a long time.

MOTEL screamed the sign on the road outside.

MOTEL called out the sign to the passing drivers.

And MOTEL cried out the sign to Christine that night three years ago after she and Mother had fought and she needed a place to take that night's John. Yes this was the answer—everything was answered. She sat with Leandra next to her, waiting. She had a John that night at seven. The clock said six thirty. She spoke idle talk to Leandra who snuggled up close and hugged Christine to her. Leandra had always been more than a friend—but suddenly, all at once, Christine rose apruptly—had she told Lewis she would be at this Motel tonight? She couldn't remember having told Lewis—and downstairs, at last, Mother reached for the balled up eviction notice and opened it out and there was the date—and had she told Lewis to meet her there?—and her Mother looked at the date, now unafraid with the Lincoln sitting outside and there came a knock on the door and there was the sound of feet outside and Christine went to the door and opened it, and it was Lewis—Lewis had come early—it almost his nickname, she laughed inside. Lewis come early. Come in, she said. Glad to see you. I must have told you.

Must have told me what? he said, stepping into her bedroom.

Oh nothing. You're here. In the right place. And at the right time. That's what counts. Come on in.

The door closed.

He looked puzzled. But, this was Christine, his Christine.

17 – Reduplicative Paramnesia

WELL, HOW DO YOU LIKE THE NEW PLACE, CHRISTINE SAID TO LEWIS.

I—what do you mean, new place?

She looked puzzled and tilted her head.

I don't mean anything Lewis. Come on. Fork it over.

He smiled as he went for his wallet.

You little devil, he said, as he pulled out three hundred dollars, and laid it on her dresser.

Did you have trouble finding the place? she said.

What do you mean finding the place? I always find the place. Are you feeling okay, Christine? I mean I've come here a hundred times. What do you mean?

Oh—yes. I don't know why, that just came out. Come on Lewis. Clothes off. Let's get down to our business.

He laughed. This was his Christine—she always said that when he got there. He took off his clothes and draped them over her chair and when he turned around, she was already under the sheets, and just like that, Lewis got into bed with her, and Christine went to work on him. And all around the Half Moon motel Christine could hear others having sex in other rooms around and below and above theirs.

Oooh, said Tanady, in the room above—you are good! You are really really good!

It was Tanady, Christine knew—Tanady's voice—he was here at the Half Moon, with somebody else. Well what did that matter as long as he kept his appointments with her. There was no reason for her to be jealous of another whore, no—but he cried out so loud that it almost drowned out the moans of Lewis and she guessed he was in the room above—and then Tanady and Lewis both cried out loud at the same time and she knew the men were both satisfied. Though she hadn't expected to hear Tanady in the room above, she asked Lewis, when they were sitting up in bed and Lewis was smoking his cigarette, Did you hear that, Lewis? Did you hear those other people having sex in the room above?

What? he said. There's no room above yours—

Oh! said Christine—I know. I don't know why I said that! Silly me—

Lewis squeezed her hand under the sheets. He knew Christine was under a lot of stress with the inspections and the threat of eviction hanging over her head. Plus she had always been a bit dizzy—a dizzy broad, but damned good, he thought to himself. He stretched out his legs under the sheets. Christine likewise stretched herself out under the sheets and then suddenly had an overwhelming urge to urinate. Excuse me, she said to Lewis, as she threw back the sheets and headed for the bathroom door. Nature calls!

Okay, he said. I'll be here, he said, smiling. He dragged on his cigarette and stubbed it out in the glass ashtray next to the bed as she headed for the bathroom door. She got in and closed the door and sat on the toilet and all at once, voices and sounds came from the room of the motel next door. She cocked her head and listened and recognized the voice as Serdon's. I usually go to Christine Zidar, he said to whoever he was with—but you are so different—so much more tender—so much calmer, someone I can really talk with, I like it.

Through the paper thin walls of the motel she heard the entire conversation and sat on the toilet for a long time, amazed.

Yes I know of Christine, said a woman's voice. She was in the nut house for years. Did you know that?

I knew she was in the hospital but you say it was the nut house?

Yes.

What exactly was wrong with her?

I don't know but she was in there for a long time. Everybody who's been to see her says she's nuts—

Christine rose, and wiped, and flushed the toilet and pulled her arm back to strike the wall with her fist and readied herself to cry out, but Leandra came up and gripped her arm and prevented her.

Christine, said Leandra. Don't do it—

But don't you hear what they are saying about me? That's a client of mine that talking over there—and he's talking about me.

Don't bang the wall and don't yell! You'll spook Lewis!

Christine relaxed her fist as Leandra continued on, what difference does it make what your clients think of you as long as they come back every week and you get your three hundred dollars and they get their good honest fuck—that's what counts— remember, that's not a man lying out there that's a three hundred dollar bill—what they think is meaningless. They're meat, that is all they are, pieces of meat—doing them is just like milking a cow. Now go back to Lewis—go back—and milk him empty. After all, he's paying you.

Christine washed her hands and cocked her head and listened
to the wall, but there was silence now. She turned and went out to
Lewis. He lay smiling on the bed, one knee up, hands behind his
head. She had never thought of him as a piece of meat before but
she guessed that was probably true. She stood staring a minute.

What? said Lewis, looking around. What's wrong?

The wall above the bed suddenly got her attention. Voices came
from behind the thin motel wall. She cocked her head and looked
past Lewis who was still waiting for an answer.

Yeah, said the voice.

It was Reinhardt. Lewis, said Christine.

What?

No, she said, raising her hand. Let me listen.

The voice said, Yeah Christine Zidar was my other whore but I
think I like you better—come on let's do it again, a growing boy
like me got's to do it again—

No! yelled Christine, bounding over Lewis and forcing him to
leap from the bed. No! she cried, as she slammed her open hand
against the wall above the bed and the sound in the hollow wall
thundered once, twice—three times and the voices finally stopped.
She knelt on the bed facing the wall, panting.

Christine, Lewis said. Christine, are you all right? What the hell
did you do that for? I'm getting out of here, you really are nuts
this time—

As he reached for his clothing Christine came off the bed and
got in front of him and said, No, don't go Lewis—I just needed
to shut them up.

Shut who up? Who? No. This is enough. Step aside, let me get
my things.

The voices in the next room—no Lewis, no—you can't leave I'll be all alone.

She tore at her hair as he struggled into his clothes.

Lord God no don't go, she cried—I'll be all alone, you are not just a piece of meat to me you are the one I like the best, you are the one I like to talk to, stay, please stay—

He paused and looked at her and said I'd love to stay Christine, but you scare me. You scared the hell out of me—what voices? What voices are you talking about?

The people all around us in all the other rooms!

There are no other rooms! This is your house! Listen—

Knowing she was about to cry, he put his hands on her shoulders and spoke into her face.

Don't cry Christine—just calm down all right? I'll stay a while—but let me get dressed now. I don't want to have sex any more tonight but I'll stay a while if that will make you happy. All right? Here—over there—go over there and put your clothes on too. Let's—let's just relax a while. Okay?

Okay.

She walked over and they both got dressed and she sat on her vanity chair and Lewis sat on the bed. It was hard for both of them to find words to say after what had just happened. Christine felt a hollow in her stomach and she knew, as Leandra had said, that Lewis was only here because he paid her to be a piece of meat. It hit her as she glanced in the mirror, with her hands quietly folded in her lap that she had no one in her life except her Mother that she could say she loved; or that loved her, just for herself. She had spent twenty years alone in the hospital surrounded by other patients and doctors and nurses, but she had been alone the whole time. And now here she was being visited by a different man each night, but she was alone the whole time. She looked over at Lewis and it was like she could see right through him. He was somehow transparent and unreal. She shifted in the chair. She had to speak to keep him from just fading to nothing.

How is your wife? she asked softly, hanging on. How is she doing these days?

My wife is fine, he said. Same old—same old.

They cracked smiles.

Still got the same job?

Oh yeah—you know, that old job—if I did something as radical as change jobs I'd tell you, you know that. You're my girl, Christine.

Your girl? What do you mean, I'm your girl?

He looked at her. What he said now was important. My girl, she whispered. Why did he say I was his girl when I'm nothing but a piece of meat—her hands trembled.

You're my girl, a good friend. We've been seeing each other for—for over two years now. Why are your hands shaking Christine? What's the matter?

She sat up straight and threw her head back. She felt that she could be honest.

I feel like a piece of meat, Lewis. It really hit me tonight here in this motel—

He rolled his eyes as she went on.

—I and so many others are just pieces of meat. We are a dime a dozen. If I disappeared tomorrow you could find a new whore to fuck, snap, just like that.

She snapped her fingers as she said that and he said, Christine, listen. First off, I'll tell you why you worry me. You say we're in a motel. But this is no motel room. We are in your house, in your room, like we always are. And second—

No! she said—we are in a room at the Half Moon motel—

He raised a hand and simply continued talking calmly and evenly.

—and second you are not just a piece of meat to me. I think of you as a friend. We've been seeing each other for so long—I think about you often and I worry about you Christine.

She glanced down at the floor. Looking back up, she spoke.

You sound like my Father.

Did you know your Father?

No. He died just after I was born. I meant you sound like what I think my father would sound like. I worry about you, you say. I suppose that's something he would have said.

That's more than something Christine.

I suppose—you know what Lewis?

No, what?

I wish I had a friend that didn't feel obliged to pay me three hundred dollars and that I didn't have to fuck every time I saw them.

Suddenly Leandra appeared next to her by the vanity and asked, What about me? Aren't I your friend?

No I mean a man friend, said Christine.

Lewis looked at her and asked her Who did you say that to?

I—I—nobody. I was just saying. I wish I had a man friend that I didn't have to fuck for money.

Maybe you should get out more, said Lewis. Go out to a bar. Have a few drinks. Kick back. You might find a friend there. Do you go to church?

Heavens, no.

That's too bad—you could go to a church function and meet a man there. You—you're beautiful Christine—you're a beautiful person. There's a man for you out there.

Do you think so? At church? Me?

Oh yeah. As a matter of fact, if I wasn't married with kids—I feel like you'd make a good wife. You'd be a great mother. I'm sure of it.

A mother? A wife? Is that me you're talking about Lewis? she said, pointing to her chest with her eyebrows raised.

Yes you, he said.

No, she thought. No never. Her gut hurt. It was no, no, never for too many things in her life. She wished to God she had never started doing this; having all these different men inside of her shooting their slimy stinking poison into her. She wished she had gone for a normal regular job. She wished she was just a normal person. Thank God she got out of that room at home, she thought. This motel room is much better.

Leandra continued to sit by her on the bed. She said Don't listen to him Christine—your life is fine. Don't let him make you think that way, that you have to be a mother or a wife to be fulfilled—he is making you have wrong thoughts. Your life is fine. You are with me, and you are with your mother—

Yes but that all is coming to an end now, she said into the air by Lewis.

He said, What? What's coming to an end? Why are you talking to no one? What is wrong Christine—I'll come right out and say it—what did they do to you in that hospital? What did they do to you in that hospital to make you do the things you do and say the things you say—first off, who were you just talking to? There's no one there.

She sat up straight. Might as well say it.

I was talking to my friend Leandra.

Leandra? There's just us two here.

No, Leandra is also here with us. Leandra is everywhere all the time.

He looked around the room. And as he looked around the room, a sound came up from under them. A voice came up from the motel room below. A voice that sounded like Mack Whiteman's. Christine cocked her head to hear.

I see Christine Zidar too, said the voice—but she's not like you. You're a lot better. I think I'll just see you from now on—I think I'll just see you, she's just a piece of meat to me, I don't care about her—

Christine clapped her hands over her ears and stood and stamped on the floor yelling Shut up! Shut up! and she stood doing this and Lewis rose and came around her and grabbed his jacket and said, I had better go—goodbye Christine—and she stamped the floor but the voice wouldn't stop and Lewis left and when the door closed behind him, the voices stopped and Leandra came and took Christine by the arm.

Christine asked Why am I cursed with this life? Why do I have such an awful life, Leandra? Lewis—where's Lewis—he ran out didn't he? Will he be coming back? He didn't say he was coming back like he usually does—and she looked at Leandra, her big sad eyes, and a freckle on the top of her nose and she threw her arms around Leandra, the last one she had besides her mother and Leandra just melted away into her, and Christine finally was all alone. She felt nothing. She felt numb. The motel rooms were all around her and they were full of voices all saying terrible things about her—they were the voices of all her Johns and she stood there listening, because she couldn't pound or stomp on all the walls, the ceiling, and the floor all at once. So she let the voices of all her Johns wash her; and as the voices were washing her clean, it came to her that she could quit her job—that she didn't have to sell herself anymore—that she was still young and that she could get a job or even go to school for something. The voices slowly changed to words of encouragement. The voices came and told her and kept coming and kept on telling her, as she stood there.

Get a job—

Quit this business—

There are things you can do, that you would be good at—

Get a job and take care of your mother—she needs you—

Go to your mother—

Go to her—

Tell her you love her—

Go to her now!

And all at once the sea appeared and great blue ice cold waves came at her from all around—and with that Christine slammed the door open and went running down the hall through the trash to go down to Thelma. She would tell Thelma she loved her, and that she forgave her. She had not said those words ever—ever before. She did not notice she was not in a motel—she did not remember where she had been—she did not know where she was—she just knew she needed to hug and kiss Thelma for the very first time; like so many times before.

18 – It's Real; it's Really, Really, Real

THELMA AWOKE IN THE RECLINING CHAIR THAT SHE ALWAYS SLEPT IN, in her nook between the mounds of trash and junk that she had collected since her husband's death. She had at last looked at the eviction notice and had gone to sleep last night knowing that it was the last night before the day that they would finally be evicted. She had slept surprisingly well, considering; she thought about Diana the inspector, and the process server in the white shirt and black tie, and she imagined that someone like that would come politely to the door, in a crisp blue suit, and say the words that had been rushing at them through the past few weeks.

Ma'am, I'm sorry. The day has come, you and your daughter have to leave—this house has been condemned. Here is the order.

It would be just like the way the officer, in his crisp blue uniform, came to tell her that her husband had died, all those years ago. And she had gone to the door with her baby Christine in her arms and the polite policeman had doffed his cap, and told her that Martin's red truck had been in an accident; a door had closed on one phase of her life in that instant; and another would open today.

Ma'am, I'm sorry. The day has come—

The officer who came and told her about Martin had gentle and caring eyes. And when he left she gently closed the door over him and over Martin and over her whole past life. She went back in the house and her life moved forward—but there would be no gentle closing of the door behind her on this one. There would be nothing more to do but go pack and leave. She and her baby Christine would go on together somewhere else.

But where God, where. Where is next? What is next?

Next was all cold, bright, and blurred over. So she turned around and finished waking and she rose and covered herself and went downstairs and, as always, she put on the water for her coffee. The small blue flame under the pot flickered slightly, as if telling her, It will all be real in a little while. It will be real when the knock on the door comes bringing the words close behind.

Ma'am, I'm sorry. The day has come—

Wreathed in the words that had not yet come she took the jar of instant coffee into her hand and spooned it into her cup. Somewhere under all the clutter was a coffeemaker that she had once used, but only God knew if she dug it up if it would it even work anymore.

Things that go unused too long die, she whispered to herself.

The house will go all unused after today.

The house will die, as Martin had died and as—

The tiny pot whistled. Her hand went to the pot and she got it and as she poured she knew the only hope left in her life was Christine in her spotless room at the very top, above all the trash. Thelma felt proud knowing Christine lay up there now, sleeping and dreaming in the spotless room Thelma had successfully defended from the trash through all the years. Christine never talked about her dreams, or about if she even had any, but Thelma imagined that they were pleasant dreams—unlike hers, so unlike hers. She put the teapot down and added milk to her cup and stirred with her one dirty spoon. The old cup she had for years lifted to her lips; she would for sure bring this cup with her. For sure she would after the words came.

Ma'am, I'm sorry. The day has come—

The mist around the words let them through a little this time, and in the words Thelma wondered how it would be to live in the car after they were evicted. Christine had said that would be how it must go; they would live in the car and get their food whatever way they could get it, and Christine had gone on and on about it all over and over every day, so at last Thelma got the eviction notice from atop the trashpile and at last read the date. Before that there had been no date because she had never seen it; because she had never looked at it, it was not real. But it was now real. She clutched her cup; who would come? When would they come?

Maybe they would not have time today, she thought as the coffee went down and the cup started to empty. Maybe she and Christine would get another day or two. Maybe—

No.

The cup went down. What time is it? She needed to know the time. She did not want them to come too early. She didn't want them to wake Christine. Baby Christine slept up in the crib. Martin was there with baby Christine in the cool and clean and quiet. What time is it? But her watch was buried, as was the clock. She could turn on the TV and get the time. But—she did not want them to come too early. She didn't want them to wake Christine. Baby Christine slept up in the crib. Martin was there with baby Christine in the cool and clean and quiet. Lord God, she had found the words to save herself—what time is it? They cannot come too early. She didn't want them to wake Christine in the cool clean quiet with Martin baby Christine with Martin all alive in the cold clean quiet—

But what is that whistling?

She reached to the stove to kill the whistling, but no. The stove was cold, not on, dead.

But that sound whistling wailing what is it what—

That's outside! My God, what's outside?

Thelma rose, kicked the underfoot trash away, clawed two trash bags down from the window, looked out, and they were there; cars; police cars, and a sheriff's car with the lights all flashing. They were here to tell her the words. The words had come.

Ma'am, I'm sorry but the day has come—

They were real, it was time, her cup fell down and as she turned from the window car doors slammed and muffled voices sounded, the creak of the step and the groan of the porch and the knock on the door. Words would come now; not those words, but words.

Police! Sheriff!

The knock on the door slammed again.

Police! Thayer County Sheriff! Open up please! We have a warrant!

No, no, no, this isn't real. They've been here before—why do they have to come here again?

Police! Thayer County Sheriff! Open up or we will force the door!

No—no. You've already told me Martin is dead. Why are you here?

Police! Sheriff—

Why are you here? I need to know why you're here. Here I come. You can't be here, you will wake my baby—

When she got to the door, it burst open before her; they had forced the door; the officer in black who had forced the door with a black battering ram stepped back and a Sherriff's deputy came in with a clipboard of paperwork, and he did not doff his cap as he had when they had come to tell her Martin was dead. There were three of them besides the one who had forced the door in, and where the door was forced the doorframe was all splintered and broken now and the dark of all the stacked trash outside had poured in around the policemen standing there and the one from the Sherriff's office, the one with the clipboard, spoke.

Are you Thelma Zidar?

The words Yes I am, came out of her.

We are here to enforce an order of eviction from Thayer County. Also is there a Christine Zidar in the house?

And again the words Yes she is, came out of her.

Where is she?

She's in her bed.

Where's her bedroom, Ma'am?

Upstairs.

We're here to arrest her for prostitution.

What?

I said—

I know what you said but what does that mean?

It means we're taking her in. Is she upstairs—God! My God. Look at this place.

The sloping, multicolored, ceiling-high mounds of garbage loomed all around them and it continued that way into the kitchen, to the steps leading upstairs which was all that was still alive of the house. The policemen and sheriff stepped in and they gazed around in amazement. As they stood there Thelma stood in their way and said Say it again, you're arresting my daughter for prostitution? What proof do you have?

She can't be a prostitute she is just a baby, a baby sleeping in her crib—

Thelma stood solidly in their way; but they pushed past her and headed down the narrow path past the kitchen, and then turned up the stairs toward the bedrooms.

No! yelled Thelma, pushing in front of them—no no no, you can't go up! You will wake Christine! Baby Christine. In her crib. With Martin there. With baby Christine—

Baby? What baby? We're going up to arrest Christine Zidar, ma'am—what are you talking about? What baby? Who the hell is Martin? Some damned John of hers? She got a John in there too? Listen, let us by so we can go up and see. Come on, just let us by—

They pushed her aside and they started up the cluttered shadowy stairs and she yelled out Christine! Christine—

Don't interfere Ma'am—don't interfere—we've got a warrant for her arrest.

Thelma pushed ahead and stood before the closed white door of Christine's room. She would not let them pass. She would not. They—they would have to kill her to get by. There were already so many dead things in the house, the whole house itself was dead, Martin was dead—what was one more thing?

No! she said to the policemen. No! You will leave her alone! Step aside—

The man in black with the battering ram was coming up the stairs.

Step aside—

The policeman shoved Thelma aside and knocked.

Police, he said loudly—Christine Zidar, open up—you're under arrest!

∞ ∞ ∞

Christine slept soundly, she never dreamed asleep. All her dreams came when she was awake. Her dreams and visions left her when she slept and her sleep was mercifully rejuvenating. But this night was different. She kept hearing shouting in her sleep. She rolled over and pulled up the covers and the dream went on.

Police! Open up—

Lewis, she said from where she sat on the vanity seat next to Leandra, who was also smiling—why don't you just come in? Don't pretend to be the police—what kind of game is this? Some big macho thing where you're going to pretend to be this big rough policeman and bust in and overpower me and fuck the shit out of me? Is that the game we're playing tonight?

Police—

And Lewis shouted through the door, this is your own fault Christine, scaring me like you did with that business about Mount Everest and all the bodies on it and how morbid that is, Christine you should be ashamed of yourself thinking anybody wants to hear such stuff, you got me so shook up I forgot to call home and say I'd be pulling an overnight, remember that I was in trouble for a long time and my wife thinks I stayed out drunk all night because of you, Christine! She thinks I'm back off the wagon and it's your fault Christine!

Christine rolled over in the bed and pulled the sheet up to her neck as she sat with Leandra laughing at Lewis, poor baby got in trouble with his wife, oh poor baby poor baby oh poor—

Police! Open up, Christine Zidar!

That's Tanady—that's Tanady's voice Leandra—hey Tanady, who are you going to be today—and who is pretending to be you today Tanady—if you play that game, you'll come busting in here like some stranger, maybe even a rapist and then you'll want to do it to me—is that how you'll get your rocks off this time? Raping me?

Tanady shouted through the door, Oh no, Christine I'm all me today and I'm going to bust into this room and you will be very sorry you gave me the business about being somebody else—what kind of damned problem do you have Christine what the hell is the matter with you?

Christine and Leandra laughed together as Tanady went on and on through the door and Christine pulled her knees up in the bed and slid off into a deeper sleep.

Police! Open up we know you're in there—

Christine perked up and her eyes closed tighter.

Serdon! Serdon, if it wasn't Lewis or Tanady it must be you Serdon, who are you going to pretend to be today? Three Nuns again?

Serdon shouted through the locked door, You're crazy Christine you know that you drive me crazy when I see you, being a good fuck isn't enough, you've got to stop saying crazy things, you've got to try and be normal or else no one will ever give a shit about you if you're not normal. Be like everybody else, like everybody else

Christine, don't be yourself, don't be crazy!

Police! Police—

She began to come slightly awake and stared at the door from the vanity chair with Leandra and they laughed and laughed at how hollow and empty the words of these Johns were, and how if Christine never saw any of these Johns again she wouldn't even care. To hell with their money, there's ways to get money—

Open up, God damn it you're under arrest—we'll break down the door, we'll break the God-damned door down—

Damn you! yelled Reinhardt through the door—you twisted my mind Christine you deserve to be arrested for what you do—you ruined me yes you ruined me, what you do is against the law after all you know—

Christine and Leandra laughed and laughed as Christine's eyes opened and she heard the loud knock at the door—

Police! One last chance before we break the door—open up, Christine—open up—

She raised her head.

Whiteman yelled through the door We'll break it down, yes we will, we'll put you in handcuffs, I was in West Point, I know right from wrong—

Leandra and Christine laughed about his prison tattoos. Who was he to say he knew right from wrong? Christine got up and backed off toward the window.

I know right from wrong Christine when you look in the mirror what you see is yourself you might not like what you see but that is you—

Open up—all right you asked for it—

Goodbye Leandra, Christine said.

Goodbye Christine. I'll see you again.

I'm sure you will.

Their hands parted.

The battering ram smashed against the door, and Christine opened the third floor window, and there it was—the peak of Mount Everest; windswept, stark, a plume of snow coming in from it. Snow and cold blew into the room, filling it. She'd always known it was there and she'd always known how she would end up—it was inevitable—the battering ram hit again and the doorframe splintered and she dove off the sill for the peak just as the police rushed in yelling, Christine don't, all her Johns' there all at once; and the abyss three stories down took her head first—she went down the hard way. There's an easy way and a hard way and she went down the hard way and she went down and hit the rocky slope below, becoming the unrecoverable body number two hundred and one; and once hit, once gone, she drifted up—a dancing imp—a new kind of a ghost that all the others had been waiting for because the two hundred other bodies frozen on the mountain had given up their imp ghosts, but now reunited, they rose with her and danced in a spiraling wreath around the mountain, the mountain which would no longer be haunted because of Christine's coming to her true home at last; a line of spirits spiraling in a single file through the cold, wind and snow, and they first made a halo on the mountain, and then they formed a crown—and at last they said farewell to Mount Everest and rose and spiraled up spinning and spreading out into space and Christine was at the head of them all, leading them out to the farthest stars, leading the way towards home forever, at last with her equals, all those frozen bodies that had been left behind, all alone, and at last all together, all at peace.

Jim Meirose is the author of three previously published novels; "Claire", "Monkey", and "Freddie Mason's Wake." Nearly three hundred of his short stories have appeared in various literary magazines and journals over the past twenty years, such as The Fiddlehead, Witness, Alaska Quarterly review, Xavier Review, New Orleans review, South Carolina Review, Whiskey Island Magazine, Ohio Edit, Bartleby Snopes, and many others. His short work has been nominated for several awards including The Shirley Jackson Award and the O. Henry Award (for which his story "Fair Morning" was short-listed). Jim lives in Somerville, NJ, with his wife, Mary Beth. Together they have one married daughter, Noelle Heber, and three beautiful grandchildren.

www.ingramcontent.com/pod-product-compliance
Lightning Source LLC
Chambersburg PA
CBHW031108260626
47172CB00001B/273